CAUGHT BETWEEN TWO BORDERS

by Richard J. Stewart

*To all my friends and family
who have had an impact on my life.*

CAUGHT BETWEEN BORDERS IN AUSTRALIA
THE CHINA CRISIS

This is a story based on events. The characters involved hold no real names. This was and is still a time when hope and tragedy for many people seemed nothing more than an everyday event, but to others, it represented a great opportunity if they had the ability to survive under extreme circumstances.

This was real and the chance for a group of friends to support each other in various states of Australia and globally.

Technology can be a good tool for communication. But these brothers and sisters went one step further. They bought and sold a tremendous amount of goods to supply not only their needs but others too.

Their friends who were isolated in different parts of the world were being supported by online trading and capitalising in precious metals that have value outweighing the destructive currency held worldwide.

When you invest in the lives of others, particularly those that have lost hope, you sow a seed of paying forward.

One of these friends had a sister involved in a tragic car accident, which left her in hospital for five months. This young woman overcame the struggles of a broken body to strive for full health. Her brother had to care for her as well as fly around the world to keep his business operational under the extraordinary events brought on by Covid.

With the highs and lows that shocked the world came laughter and joy for the brothers and sisters who got on with their lives.

I'm reminded daily, "Going to church don't make you a Christian, going to McDonald's don't make you a hamburger."

With the help and inspiration of these brothers and sisters, the story unfolds through businesses and private lives from east to west in Australia.

I would incorporate a good friend as well. He has acted behind the scenes as a financial businessman of Perth and has contributed his wisdom on many occasions and been helpful in providing work and accommodation when needed as part of this story. Without his provisions, things could have got a little messy.

And of course, a thank you to my own family—my wife, two daughters, my surviving mother in New Zealand, and Ronald and Jemma who have been in contact with us right the way through as encouragement and a listening ear.

There are many others we could thank, from major businesses and private individuals.

To anyone reading this story, no real names will be given but the consistency of factual events will remain.

Also, you will find many of the people in the story never quit when the going got tough, when a group of other people were trying to manipulate and destroy economies causing fear to many nations.

I hope you enjoy this story and appreciate everyone is on a different journey in this life given to us. We should make the best out of every opportunity that blesses others, not destroy human dignity.

Richard J Stewart.

THE FLIGHT
TO NEW ZEALAND

Work had been pretty hectic for Ricky in the year leading up to a new decade. 2019 had been no different—he was working long hours on mining operations in Queensland, Northern Territory and Western Australia. It had taken a toll: the cost of time traveling, those long hours combined with working in those extreme conditions, the heat, the flies, the continual maintenance of staying hydrated and keeping a professional approach to work on various high and technical machinery onsite. Many of his colleagues who worked alongside Ricky appreciated his helpfulness and consideration towards them. Most of all, his sense of humour made something funny out of every situation and helped them keep their sanity.

It was that time of the year on the west and east coast of Australia with extreme heat and meteorological conditions that can generate tropical cyclones with heavy flooding and severe lightning storms. Every building had to be secured and every item in the lay down yards secured either by webbing or hold down pins in case of code Red and Yellow alerts. During a Red alert, work stopped immediately, and employees had to seek safe allocated buildings to take shelter in. During Yellow, all mining operations stopped.

Rick knew what it was like to be trapped in heavy flooding and severe lightning storms in a mining vehicle, nearly being swept away under the extreme pressure of water, having no place to turn but simply go with the current. The road had been washed out that night going back to the camp. The fellas in the vehicle preceding had got through without realising how bad the water levels had risen behind them. Ricky and three others were in a meter of rising water.

Calmly, Ricky fought the current and saw some high ground directly in front. If he could just get some traction in the Toyota four-wheel drive, there was a chance of driving up a stop bank.

Prior to this, Ricky was thinking about his well-deserved holiday with family and friends in New Zealand. He was flying out the next day. His wife Victoria and two daughters Renae and Paula had flown out two days prior and were waiting for Ricky to join them two days before Christmas that year at his mother's place in Matamata, New Zealand.

Now with three other fellas in the Ute, petrified things could get ugly, he knew this was his only chance to reach safety. This he calmly did. The front tyres gripped first and then slid left and right. The back tyres started to get traction. They drove up and over the stop bank, making it to a safe area.

Immediately and calmly, Mick in the passenger's seat radioed mining emergencies on the mine's emergency channel, advised the location, the emergency, the number of persons affected and what was needed to get them out.

"Emergency emergency emergency, Mick Stanton speaking, mining vehicle trapped in high flooding on mining road to camp facilities. Four persons on board, require immediate assistance. We have been able to make it to higher ground above the high level of water. Two persons in a state of shock."

Mick checked to make sure everyone else was ok, advising we had reached higher ground and emergency services had been contacted as to the location. A GPS tracker had also been installed in the mining Ute as

conditions in very remote areas of Australia can be severe.

There was no response as to the fellas in the back, who were pale white and in a state of shock.

The water would rise even further with the cyclone developing more intensely that night, but they were safe for now, waiting for help.

Ricky was reminded of Forrest Gump: "Mumma says life is like a box of chocolates, you never know which one you are going to get."

Ricky and Mick and the other two fellas were very thankful as they could have been completely swept away to who knows where or even have been wrapped around a tree in the middle of nowhere. Someone high up was looking after them.

This wasn't the only thing they had to deal with. Although mining emergency had their GPS position and would arrive as soon as the water levels and extreme weather eased, disorientated wildlife was crashing into the vehicle in the dark. Kangaroos, even a snake, appeared on the bonnet of the Toyota. When daybreak came, they could hear some more banging on the base of the vehicle. When Rick looked to the side of the vehicle, he saw a two-and-a-half-meter croc lying near the tray and back tyre. Now they would certainly not get out of the vehicle.

All Ricky and Mick could think was that a prehistoric monster had temporarily found lodging at the base of a Toyota light vehicle.

Mining emergency would have to contact a park ranger as well and would have to fly in by chopper.

The fellas in the back seemed to have come alive in the early morning. Joel's first words were "Where are we?" And when he looked out and saw the two-and-a-half-meter croc, he exclaimed, "What the heck?"

The worst of the weather was passing and there was still the wind to deal with. The water levels were slowly receding although it would take another three or four days for water levels to completely drop.

There was no other option but for mines emergency to have a chopper flown in to get everyone flown out. At some later date, a recovery team would come and get the vehicle.

A call on the radio came through from mine emergency. A chopper would be on its way within the hour.

Fortunately, they had enough fuel in the vehicle to keep the engine running and the electrics charged, so radio comms were not a problem.

Apparently, they had sailed down the waterlogged road about one hundred kilometres with the fast-moving water. When Rick looked around and saw all the debris and trees floating, he was surprised the Toyota had not been wrapped around any of them. The old sturdy Toyota had lived up to its rugged reputation once again.

It was about 5.30 a.m. Rick had to be on that mining charter flight back to Perth and then catch the 11.30 p.m. flight back to Queensland by mid-afternoon and the chopper was nowhere to be seen. Mining emergency had advised chopper was airborne an hour ago and still no sign.

Mick, Joel, and Dan were starting to get a little edgy with a lack of sleep, the limited amount of water, and hunger pains setting in. It didn't help with the croc positioned against the side of the Ute either. Provoking this big thing to move would not be a good idea either.

What did follow was something very interesting. An indigenous man gathering native plants for herbal extracts had been caught on high ground from the previous night's flooding. He had come on the scene from amongst the trees and had seen their predicament.

Most mining operations are on indigenous land and they have a responsibility and obligation under the environmental act to maintain and repair land in use and return it in good condition to the

❋

local people. The local people are also the custodians of the land and royalties are paid to them through negotiations with the mining companies.

This man knew the land and the wildlife and came to our rescue with the croc predicament. In some strange way, he must have been the croc whisperer as not long after he did his chanting, the croc moved from the muddy bank next to the Ute tyre, sliding into the water.

When Rick asked him what he did to move the croc along, he just said, "I told the croc the best food is in that direction," and the croc moved on. Not sure if he was having Rick and Micky on or he really believed it but just like he came from nowhere, he disappeared back into the bush.

Rick reminded himself of a blonde joke in contrast to Mr Croc Whisperer.

There was a blonde lady on a flight one day flying from Perth to the UK. The blonde woman had taken a seat she hadn't paid for in business class and when confronted by the cabin crew, she would not move.

"Miss, you haven't paid for this seat, you cannot sit here."

A reply came back adamantly. "I'm not moving."

The cabin crew immediately went to see the captain of the aircraft who promptly came down to defuse the situation. He whispered something in the blonde lady's ear and she immediately got up and moved herself to the seat allocated to her.

A stunned hostie asked the captain, "What did you say to her?" His reply was, "I told her this part of the plane was not going to London."

A simple whisper in someone's ear or chant, in this case a croc, can sometimes make a person or a reptile hear what they want to hear. May not be factual but it tickles their ears.

This was a funny ha ha experience for Rick and his colleagues. It would make a talking point back at the camp.

The chopper did arrive not long after the indigenous man disappeared back into the bush. When asked where the croc was, the men had a laugh and pointed in that direction. "He's gone fishing."

Rick was reminded of being grateful of no fatalities and in his heart thanked God for his protection.

A check by the medics on Rick, Micky, Dan and Joel showed they had not been emotionally stressed out by the previous night's events and after having a good meal, they were driven to the mine's airport.

The chartered flight would land in the next hour and the team would be on board, with hopefully an uneventful flight back to Perth.

For Rick it would be another eight hours on two connecting flights before he was back in Mackay, Queensland and he was looking forward to it. Micky, Dan, and Joel were based in Perth. Rick, like many other east coasters, floated between states, an expense sometimes picked up by the companies he worked for or else Rick paid for the travel to Perth himself.

Nonetheless Rick would make a quick turn around and within a day would be in Auckland, New Zealand, followed by a two-hour minivan trip from Auckland International Airport to the big smoke of Matamata, Hobart Town from *Lord of the Rings*.

START EVERY DAY WITH A SMILE
AND GET OVER IT

Rick and the gang had mounted the steps of the B737 Qantas charter aircraft and had taken their seats. A two-hour flight to Perth, a snooze on the way, maybe some loud-mouthed miners having come off a night shift but they would be on their way within twenty or so minutes.

Rick closed his eyes just thinking of the night before. Completely oblivious to the cabin crew talking and the captain's brief on flight time to Perth, he fell asleep. The two hours had gone very quickly and he was still in a state of unconsciousness for the descent into Perth International with the cabin crew giving the pre-landing briefing, a very familiar routine from many a flight flown.

DON'T LOSE HOPE.
THERE'S ALWAYS SOMETHING GOOD COMING.
REMEMBER THAT.

When the cabin crew were giving the emergency briefing for the emergency exit row, Rick loved waiting for the cabin to finish then ask, "Have you ever had to do the emergency procedure in real life?" The answer always came back indignantly "no" as if to say, "You shouldn't ask those questions." Rick always had a chuckle. He knew what would involve a real emergency as he had been exposed to several in the air.

He landed in Perth and wished his colleagues a safe and happy Christmas, wondering what Christmas really meant to them, also thinking what would Christmas have really been like for their families and his own if the police had had to turn up to each spouse's door, having to pass the dreadful news that their husband or partner had drowned in a mining catastrophe due to flooding.

Then Rick remembered he had a connecting flight. The flight would not leave for another five hours. Dropping his bags in a lock up, he preceded to the Qantas club for a shower and a meal. This night would be a long wait as electrical storms were heavily populating above the eastern states and east coast of Western Australia. This would mean a delay in return flights from Perth to Brisbane and possibly missing connecting flights back to Mackay. If flights were delayed and connecting flights were missed, Qantas would put you up in a hotel and taxi you back to the airport for the first connecting flight next day.

In between times, Rick had phoned his business friend in Perth who had flown in from Singapore the day before. Jimmy had building properties all over Perth, from commercial to apartments. As a successful engineering contractor in Perth, he had done extremely well from humble beginnings. It was always great for Rick to catch up with him and his office staff as they would go out for a meal or coffee and talk about real life issues. The accommodation he had provided for Rick and his friends on flying in and out of the western states to the east coast was very reassuring. Sometimes Rick would even help Jimmy when his labour force, especially when the electrical contractors, were extremely busy.

Rick was always in the trading business and while he was in Perth there was something more valuable than currency he needed to purchase for events he knew would be coming to pass. He wasn't sure what, but history had a way of repeating itself and those who control a system to basically manipulate human life as we know were always going to do something sinister. There was Rick, Paul, James, Graeme, Michelle, and Georgie on this side of the continent who had banded together against an all-out right assault on a world basis. No one would ever believe what the forces of evil were preparing to do. People seemed unaware, uninterested, unprepared. You could call it a form of complacency, apathy maybe, as most people wouldn't want to believe their bubble could be burst. And that's why the team started to build under these circumstances.

Rick brought what he needed back home to Mackay.

There was something going to unfold in the next few months that the world was not prepared for.

Someone said governments are always ready to diffuse a nuclear disaster, but are never fully prepared for an all-out biological war, with consequences that would wipe out millions of vulnerable people.

Did Rick know something that many did not know was coming?

This would be a new journey for Rick, gaining positive mentorship from other successful people like Jimmy and at the same time thinking about just having that break over the Christmas period he needed with his wife and two grown girls in New Zealand. In all this time, it gave Rick time to think.

11.30 p.m. came that Thursday night and there was no Airbus at the loading air bridge. As presumed, the weather at this time of the year caused havoc.

Rick was always wondering why the company wouldn't provide a private jet to fly their staff in and out of these mines. You wouldn't have to wait around airports and you could avoid serious weather and be home quicker. But this was just a dream as he prepared to slowly change his vocation.

The Airbus did fly into Perth, and included a late turn around. It was a four-and-half to five-hour flight back to Brisbane, with a correctional time difference of two hours between the states.

He hoped to get some sleep in those five hours, although trying to get comfortable in a seat on an aircraft can be quite difficult.

The hours went quickly. He had flown this route often. You board the plane, you sleep into the night hoping you don't have a chronic snorer next to you, you wake to the east coast sunshine as the plane descends, you listen to the cabin crews briefing on the pre-landing cabin checks, you land and you disembark. That's the best you hope for.

Sometimes you meet people on these flights you know and sometimes you chat with people dying to have a conversation.

On this particular flight, a lightning strike during the night had hit the right-hand trailing edge of the airbus right wing. The crew was unaware till the light of morning sun shone on a heavily blackened area of the wing.

Rick could see some sustained damage from his seat and point-ed it out to the crew. A few other passengers had made the same observation and were a little concerned. The captain was immedi-ately notified as no control systems or avionics had any sustained damage.

The Qantas Airbus A330 was in its descent phase within a half hour of making a final approach into Brisbane International Airport.

The captain came and made a brief observation. It was fortunate that the lightning strike had not been close to the fuel tanks and although the discharging current points had done their job, the damage made by the strike was a little concerning. The captain would have to report the visible damage to the engineers on the ground. The two would be inspecting the severity of the damage and the repairs necessary.

The aircraft did land safely with a gaping hole towards the rear of the right-hand wing. Emergency services had been notified and were on standby just in case the aircraft had problems in the approach and landing phase.

The week had ended full of excitement for Rick and his colleagues Mick, Joel, Dan: being stranded, having nearly been washed away from a mining road and a swollen river, and now this. Rick asked himself what was next, in anticipation.

They landed and all passengers were rushed off the Airbus through the airbridge on to the concourse so aircraft engineers could move aircraft off the airbridge to the hangars for major inspections on the wing surface, checking the intergradation of wing spars for damage.

Rick knew what it was like to be caught in his own aircraft in a storm, pelted with hail, up and down droughts and having been thrown around violently before he could fly the aircraft through and outside the storm cell. A mayday call nearly eventuated. After landing his aircraft, the aircraft had to be checked thoroughly for structural, mechanical, and electrical damage.

Meanwhile Rick headed towards the Qantas flight service desk along with another supervisor he had worked with on the west coast, having to rearrange flight details. Flights had also been delayed due to lightning activity over Brisbane the night before. The airport had to be closed on a blue alert level, reopening a few hours later.

There were a lot of people exasperated that day and a few CHOICE WORDS used. However, it wasn't that late in the day and Rick and Brian, on their connecting flight to Mackay on the Queensland eastern coast, would only be delayed for three hours before a Qantas link flight would leave and get them on the ground at Mackay by mid-morning 23rd December.

Brian was ex-military and a special forces serviceman. He had seen some of the most horrific scenes in Iraqi and Afghanistan and counselling had been needed on his return to Australia for over-come the stress and trauma he went through. Brian was a leader and good at his supervisory roll-on mining machinery. He was one of the fortunate servicemen who was looked after on return from active service. He had the feeling that he was appreciated and cared for as he also tried to fit back into family and civilian life. Like Rick's good friend Johnny who had been a warrant officer in the New Zealand Army and later in active service in the private sector of the Iraqi conflict, Johnny, a Māori war hero, would not divulge what he had seen in his three tours, but had needed to talk about certain things that had troubled him on his return to Australia.

Rick and Brian would chat for hours over a coffee and breakfast at the Qantas lounge until their flight departed Brisbane to arrive at the Mackay airport. This would be a well-deserved break. Shaking hands, they wished each other a safe and happy holiday.

An Uber driver drove Rick home to his apartment at 5 Donning Ton Street. As no one would be home, he asked the driver if he would wait fifteen minutes so he could shower, change, and quickly fill a suitcase with everything he needed for the New Zealand trip. This was ok with the driver. Rick didn't believe in tips but he wasn't going to let the driver go emptyhanded for waiting those extra few minutes.

Again, Rick would have to fly from Mackay to Brisbane on the turbo prop aircraft he had come back on an hour and a half before. Packed and ready to go, Rick locked up the house, ran across the lawn, and jumped into the Uber Toyota Prado. The last thing on Rick's mind was any delays now on the road or at the Mackay and

Brisbane airport.

The Uber driver dropped Rick off at the car drop off point. Rick gave the fella an extra fifty dollars for his services. Rick looked at his watch. It was now 12.30 p.m. His flight would leave at 1.15 p.m. for Brisbane and the international flight to New Zealand 4.40 p.m. AEST departure.

In New Zealand in the last year, two major tragedies had unfolded. The first was a lone gunmen went out on a rampage, firing a number of rounds from a semi-automatic gun into two mosques in Christchurch, killing a number of innocent victims and seriously injuring a number of others before two police officers apprehended him. Amongst the dead were men, women, and children. New Zealand was in a state of shock for a number of weeks.

The second tragedy happened at the end of 2019 when a number of tourists on a cruise liner from Australia were taken by boat on an excursion trip to an active volcanic island off the east coast of the North Island, when it violently exploded, killing over twenty people.

Rick knew the areas of Christchurch, New Zealand where the shooting had taken place as he had lived and worked there several years ago.

And Rick had also flown private charter flights around the volcanic island that had erupted on several occasions. His home base was forty nautical miles off the east coast of the North Island.

If you like outdoor extreme adventure, New Zealand is the place to go. Yes, sometimes it might be a little dangerous, but from the snow-topped mountains, to the rivers, lakes, active volcanoes, the beaches, the surf, the greenery, the fishing and so on, the oasis at the bottom of the world was extreme fun. But as like any other place in the world, it had its dangers.

The people Rick had cared for over the years were his family, his close friends, sponsored World Vision children on three continents of the world, two Australian school children who needed support with their education, the Royal Flying Doctors, and a few others. He figured many people had given him and his siblings a head start in life. Investing in younger people to have the same advantages in life was something he was passionate about.

As for the Royal Flying Doctors, Rick had been flown out from a mining camp to a hospital and he never forgot what the doctors and nurses did to save his life that night.

Rick always thought a flying career would be the ultimate, but he was focused now with his mentor friends Jimmy and Earl, both with two different backgrounds but highly successful. They would drive him to build an ongoing asset to free his time up for family, friends and people he really cared for.

The boarding call came for QF 945 departing Brisbane for Auckland, New Zealand. On that same flight was one of the pilots Rick had recognised. Elton Forbe was his name and he had risen to the position of first officer on the Airbus A330. Elton was also a Kiwi (New Zealander) but had joined the Qantas ranks after some redundancies with Air New Zealand a year prior. Elton didn't know what the coming year would bring for the existence of every world airliner nor the devastating effects on countries' economies.

As Rick was boarding, he asked the cabin crew if they would pass on a personal message to Elton.

In his early years, Rick had always called Elton Elton John. Not the rocket man, he was the Qantas man now. He wasn't a boom boom ciao either. Elton wasn't the charismatic singer as Elton John but he could still sing and hold an audience. It seemed Rick had a nickname for all his friends, and nicknames or cover names would be useful in the future for a team.

If Elton knew Rick was on the flight, he would certainly have made a point of contacting him. Elton was as good a friend as any other Rick had. They had gone to the same school, played the same sport, were in Air Cadets and Scouts, and had travelled together, but eventually their vocations had been in different directions. One thing they were passionate about was the aviation industry.

Rick had gained his professional licence whilst achieving his trade and electrical technician licences, whilst Elton pursued mechanical engineering and advanced aviation studies. The fact remained that Elton was still part of the brotherhood and this would become prevalent in what happened in the months to come.

The doors were closed, the cabin crew had commenced their departure brief as the Airbus A330 was pushed back, and the crew were starting the turbines. The captain would make calls on the PA as to time of arrival in Auckland and give the usual information about weather along the way and of course the old "sit back and relax, thanking you for flying Qantas" as the airbus taxied to the holding point.

Rick was strapped in and the weariness he felt was causing his eyes to close as he drifted off into a deep sleep. Sleeping in an aircraft seat is not the most comfortable place to sleep, but if your body slumps into unconsciousness in a deep sleep, nothing matters.

When you are flying east to west over any large continent like Australia, the time differences can be anywhere between one to two to three hours difference. From east to west, you are losing time, whereas west to east, you are gaining time and jet lag can follow. And if you don't allow for the correction on your watches (these days some watches and cell phones change automatically), you can get caught out on time differences, especially if you have set your alarm for work. Two hours early can make a big difference to your sleep pattern if you know what I mean.

So began the holiday for Rick. The hours from lack of sleep had caught up with him as he slept the three-hour journey across the Tasman Sea. He had missed out on meals in unconscious sleep and as the A330 Airbus prepared to make the approach into Auckland International and the announcements in preparation for landing were made by the cabin crew, Rick was still fast asleep. Elton, the first officer, made the formal announcements about Auckland conditions from the flight deck and wished everyone a safe and happy Christmas. Using a semi-code, he also greeted his good friend

Rick and said that the flight deck needed attention; in other words, when everyone else had disembarked, Rick should come down to the flight deck. Rick's note had gotten through to Elton.

The A330 Airbus made a perfect landing, the time now 11.30 p.m. It would take a few minutes for aircraft to taxi to air bridge and for passengers to disembark.

Rick was still asleep in his chair and at this point would be the last to leave as he was sitting in a window seat. As the airbridge was connected, the seat belt sign disengaged. People jumped up from seats to retrieve their personal belongings, and then wait for the door to open.

Elton had established what seat Rick had been sitting in and as he hadn't heard from him, he waited for everyone to leave and walked down the aisle to find Rick as he hadn't left with all the other passengers.

There he was, still asleep. Elton gave him a gentle nudge. Rick groggily opened his eyes and turned to see a smiling Elton. Getting his thoughts together, Rick asked, "What happened, where is everyone, Elton buddy?"

With a smile on his face, Elton said, "You're the last to leave, sleeping beauty, come with me and we'll get through customs quick, you got your paperwork?"

Rick grabbed Elton's hand, pulled himself up, grabbed his kit from the overhead locker and followed Elton through the doors of the aircraft and up the airbridge, talking as they went. Then up through terminal across, down through customs, passports and documents of entry handed over, bags checked through scanners.

Elton had brought Rick with him through the crew customs scanner and then out through the front door of the airport exit.

"Elton man, I am so glad to see you. If I had known you were going to be on this flight, I would have contacted you in advance."

"Rick, everything is so security tight, even our rosters could be changed at a moment's notice. I got this horrible feeling something not so good is going to happen in the New Year. Can't give you all the details but some Asian countries have kept quiet about a serious virus that's killing people and because of this, many airlines around the world are on alert."

"Come on, Elton, this is Christmas, you are becoming a bit paranoid."

"No, I'm serious, man."

"Elton, you got transport to drop me off at the shuttle bus pickup point?"

"I'm with the crew, mate. I am only doing an overnighter, flying to Sydney in the morning. We have to stay together as of company policy."

"Elton, I'm on break for two weeks with my mother, wife, and two girls. Can we catch up in Brisbane on my return?"

"We will make a plan."

Though neither knew it at the time, in the New Year, Elton would become a part of the brothers and sisters helping out with friends who would be restricted from traveling between borders in Australia and overseas. Elton would also be stood down from his pilot's position as Qantas would be laying off twenty thousand employees.

Elton shook Rick's hand and gave Rick a brotherly hug as they said their farewells.

It was then this thought came to Rick: *Don't wish it were easier, wish you were better.*

THE NEW ZEALAND HOLIDAY

KILOMETRES ARE SHORTER THAN MILES.
SAVE GAS AND TAKE THE NEXT TRIP IN KILOMETRES.

Finding the pre-booked shuttle bus waiting at the other side of the international terminal, Rick clambered on board with a few other weary travellers for his two-hour ride to Matamata, a Māori name given to the small bustling farming township in the Waikato province. This was a time when crazy drivers were on the road, but in all this, Rick always had a thankful attitude for God's provisions.

Living out of Qantas lounges and travelling thousands of kilometres on the road, Rick knew that he believed in a higher power that watched over him day and night.

Rick was finally able to say he was beginning his holiday. His daughters Renae and Paula would pick up the rental car hired from a private company in Matamata and would be ready to travel around the North Island of New Zealand in the coming weeks. His wife Victoria would be preparing a curry munch (Indian meal) for Rick on his arrival. His lovely mother whom Rick had only seen a year ago in a transit flight to Thailand with Renae would be so looking forward to seeing Rick, her youngest son, and having those wonderful days with the whole family over Christmas.

There was something troubling Rick, although this was the time of year for celebrating the events of Christmas. This hunch would play out in months to come.

Then he had a forty-minute road trip over the hill from Matamata into Tauranga by car.

Rick and Victoria and his two lovely daughters spent a few days with Grandma.

Rick had grown up with his siblings further east. He would always reminisce over the stable family he grew up in and the people who encouraged him to pursue his God-given dreams. Some of those wonderful people had passed on now but he could still remember the words of wisdom they would share.

IN HIS HEART A MAN PLANS HIS COURSE,
BUT THE LORD DETERMINES HIS STEPS.
—Proverbs 19:2

One thing that was on Rick's mind whilst he was in New Zealand was to pick up all of his father's photo albums and memorabilia. His father had passed away fifteen months before and he longed to keep that connection with both his parents alive.

Rick also knew there had been a family history book that had disappeared and legend had it that family tree went right back to Robert the Bruce, the ancient King of Scotland. Where could this book be?

Rick's mother had the remaining albums from his grandparents who had passed on a few years earlier but nothing to show off his Scottish legacy. His mother was English and had been married to a descendant of Scottish ancestry, the pride that held up the Royal name of Scotland, the clan that would lead the Scots against the English over two hundred years ago from the highlands to their unfortunate defeat at Culloden.

History, events, and people were always on Rick's mind. His close friends on both sides of the Tasman would remain loyal to him as he was to them. They had good values, unheard of in this day and age. However, there would be a growing number of people quietly re-affirming good values to stand together as the events would unfold in the next year.

A new expressway had been built on the other side of the Mount going east. And unfortunately, road tolls went with it. Further east towards a place called Whakatane, Rick could see the steaming

 volcanic island (White Island) about twenty-five kilometres off the coast that had killed those Australian tourists and charter operators a few weeks earlier and he re- membered how he had taken people out there on air charters.

He drove a little further with three women in the car. They stopped and got out and Rick just sat with his eyes closed for a few minutes, thinking of his five-year plan to kick some real goals. Rick had read, had listened, had been mentored, and whilst he was on holiday with the renewing of his mind in a relaxed atmosphere, he was beginning to formulate plans on how a group of people on both sides of the Tasman were going to protect themselves, their fami- lies, their friends and many others in trouble if and when this empire of bad people at the top of the world food chain would attempt to distort and destroy the economies of this world. How did Rick know this? Rick had been studying a series of events over a number of years and also the parallels from Biblical Revelations where proph- esies had actually started to come true.

Many people had been fooled worldwide of the state of each country's economy and the trading of currencies (not real money, just paper and figures).

He had a plan just like the professor at the electrical engineering school had taught him.

"Son, you must have a plan for every detail for any event you plan, every detail that could go right, and every detail that could go wrong. Secondly, you must study that plan and teach it to everyone else on the team and make sure they know every move.

"Thirdly, you must be one step above your opponent, knowing every decision they are going to make and how you plan to coun- teract that decision before they even make it."

The professor had not only taught Rick the fundamentals of electrical engineering, but the ability to create and design your life with the ability to involve others.

Those few minutes sitting in the car with his eyes closed and his thoughts in motion had given him peace of mind.

There was a banging on the window. "Come on, Dad, we are outside having some fun and you're in the car with your eyes closed."

Rick got out of the car and as he did, a ball came flying towards him. He booted that ball in the direction of Renae. The game was on. Renae and Paula and a few others had joined in a game of soccer.

So the game was on. In soccer or in any other game where you have a team, your players are positioned according to their abilities.

You have a captain or someone in charge to lead the team, you have those who are positioned in the front line or play forward to maintain the charge, you have two wing men who can position themselves to score a point when the opposition drops their guard, then you have the mid fields-men or women who are there when the game is brought back into your field of play, then comes the backs that protect the heart of the operation in your field of play, and an intern who protects the operation's centre or the goalkeeper to prevent opposition knowing the next move.

And then there was always the plan B, the back-up plan to confuse the opposition when he thinks he has you in his sights but you outsmart him to put you in front again.

The Kenny Rogers song, "The Gambler," once again came into Rick's mind, how a gambler shouldn't count his money when other people are watching.

A few years ago, Rick had done one of his last chartered flights in New Zealand, flying across Lake Taupo, central North Island, flying above the military playground where the New Zealand Army played their war games. Remembering the lakes and where they were now on holiday gave Rick some more ideas for a team.

The year of 2019 was quickly coming to an end. The year 2020 was about to be broken in.

The last four years had brought in a promising leader in North America who loved his country and people, and stood up for injustice at vengeance and distaste of his rivals. A very dangerous place to be in as accusations and trumped-up charges would try and remove him from office, while he brought the economy and border protection back into shape.

Rick had studied and learned that the so-called world powers were trying to remove him from office so they could keep their agenda intact. The year 2020 would be a start of their horrific plan.

In New Zealand, the preparations for the New Year's celebrations were about to begin. Fireworks off the harbour bridge, the food, the singing, the dancing, the partying.

The time of reflection on holiday would last the two weeks Rick and family were in New Zealand. Many of his goals had been achieved in New Zealand in his younger years between the 1970s and mid-1980s and then everything changed. The government of the day sold off state assets, making people redundant from so called unprofitable government departments and making the dollar value more important than people. The government made huge profits at the expense of people's lives.

Rick had seen the downside of this where he worked in rural areas of NZ. The poverty, the mental health issues, government dole cheques and to top it off, the increase in producing drugs. Rick flew over drug related areas to work and there were times he saw flashes of light as if someone was firing rifle ammunitions at him.

That was the downside of New Zealand.

Across the Tasman, there was not much difference but a bigger economy and huge deposits of natural resources. Farming held a big portion of the economy together but the inefficiencies also existed in Australia, Rick's adopted country and a country he loved as well as New Zealand.

The holiday was coming to an end. Rick hadn't managed to see his brother who lived further south and his younger sister who lived in Dallas, Texas but there would be a next time.

One of Rick's daughters had left early for Australia for work commitments and now Rick and Victoria would leave the same way as they had come, by shuttle bus to Auckland and flying back to Mackay via Brisbane. Renae would stay for a time before coming back to Australia. Rick would say goodbye to his mother and promised he would see her in the new year. But that would not happen due to what was coming.

Rick was building his team and this team was going to be ready for what was to come and stand for what was right. It was a team that would band communities together, but would also give back what had been taken from them and that was self-worth.

So Rick and Victoria would arrive back in Australia. Victoria was training for a fundraiser marathon for the victims of the Christchurch massacre in early March 2020. This is where the story starts.

TEAM BUILDING

Rick had come to realise some years back that the governments around the world had lied to the people of every nation. Career politicians had exploited and mismanaged their own financial systems intentionally for a higher power. Resources of many countries had been taken over because the interest for world banking loans could not be paid. Pension funds had been stolen by these very same people and people were being led blindly to their demise thinking their own nation's leaders had their own best interests at heart. We are a democracy, are we not?

Higher taxes, rampant inflation, mortgage sales, all were coming due to the huge borrowing because of a so-called pandemic internationally. Rick had to build this team. The communities of Australia needed hope to reverse what had been stolen over time. The international agency run by the three thousand elite must be exposed and this was just the beginning.

To be a team player, there would some rules you had follow.

- First, mutual respect for each other. Only those who could be trusted and work together in difficult situations would be considered. And some of those persons would not have much in a worldly sense but had various skills that were important.
- Code names would be given. They would need a network of communications able to disenfranchise themselves from any government spy network or global tracking system.

- They needed to be in good physical shape and be
  semi-trained in medical emergencies.
- They would also need to get off the grid.
  Not disappear but become anonymous.
- Nothing should ever be discussed outside the circle.
- Training in a classroom format would be given from
  an unidentifiable premise with no loose ends left.
- Finally, they would assign a field leader who would be
  responsible for the comings and goings of persons.

COURAGE DOESN'T ALWAYS ROAR.
SOMETIMES COURAGE IS A LITTLE VOICE
AT THE END OF THE DAY THAT SAYS,
"I'LL TRY AGAIN TOMORROW."

This was now January 2020. The virus that started in China had mutated around European cities and a coverup was just beginning.

The virus attacked people's immune systems and their lungs, causing people's lungs and organs to shut down. People were starting to die in the thousands and this was just the start worldwide.

Flights were being stopped into the U.S. from China. The virus had viciously attacked Italy, Spain, Germany, the Baltic countries and then spread through France, Belgium, the Netherlands and the UK. The last flights were being assigned to get expats back to their own countries, but this would come at a huge financial cost as well as a physical cost. The virus would be transported globally and there seemed no way of stopping it.

Borders were being closed. Hospitals were being swamped with people suffering and dying. Temporary field hospitals were set up and countries were quarantining persons with the virus.

This virus had come from China but the regime was trying to cover up warnings from their own medical people.

The world was suffering from an epidemic like nothing ever seen before.

Families were displaced, world economies were in disarray. Thousands of jobs were lost, placing an enormous financial burden on governments as they created bailouts for those struggling to survive job loss and financial hardship.

Rick's friend Elton was given the news he would be stood down and a number of his other close friends were in the same position.

But Rick and his friends had a plan, that plan would involve some of the team who had been trapped overseas and the resources they were able to help them with.

Everyone has a history. What you do with it is up to you.
Some repeat it.
Some change it.
Some learn from it.
The real special ones use it to help others.

Here in Australia the panic to close borders was about to start. This caused major disruptions interstate.

THE PLAN

So stage one began. Rick had purposely stayed back in Mackay to secretly set up the operations centre in a rundown warehouse. He could coordinate from there or remotely.

Rick would use the code name Alpha.

Elton would be Foxtrot the computer Wizz.

Jimmy would be called Delta. Jimmy brought with him the finance and not what you know but who you know aspect.

Brian the mining supervisor had agreed to take charge of the field leadership and he would be called Lima. He knew how to infiltrate signals and play both defensive and offensive when it came to facing the enemy. The enemy would be those who were stealing human rights and manipulating the world's resources.

Paul, code name Charlie, agreed to become a mobility expert, finding transport from motorcycles to old cars that would leave no trace of identities.

Michelle, code named Zulu, architecturally designed tunnels if and when needed to evacuate people to safe areas.

Georgia, code name Tango, was brilliant at facial disguises and was able to mix in with any groups without being recognised.

We had a slight problem with Graeme, code name Romeo, who had come with us but was dealing with his sister's hit and run and hospitalisation in Sydney. He would be online comms each day.

His import export business would bring in cash to help purchase all equipment from machinery to technology. He was having to fly to New Zealand where consignments had been shipped to the wrong country only to find it was the wrong consignments.

He then of course had to fly to Turkey where the consignments were shipped from to find he had to pay extra for the mistake they had made and to pay extra for shipping and customs costs. This shipping company would not acknowledge their mistake and sorting the costs out would be left to Romeo.

Sorting this out and managing his sister's operations in hospital came at considerable cost.

As he was part of the team, the team managed to consistently help with the medical bills and accommodation and consignment expenses as the costs would be retrieved from what was coming back into Australia.

The costs would be only a small amount considering what was coming into the operation. This was precisely what the team was setting up for, and this was the first venture the team would aid in.

There were many expats stuck in every continent of the world. The Australian government was doing its best by contracting Qantas Airbus A380 and Boeing 747s to fly out expats but the flights would not be enough. Some of the other airlines were charging thousands upon thousands of dollars to fly persons and families home and some people would not make it home for many months.

Then came the quarantine. Each country was setting up its two-week mandatory quarantine. And then came the lockdowns and every business except essential services would stop.

Victoria had planned the running event and to meet up in Christchurch, New Zealand with other runners, running the fifty-two mile course (miles not kilometres) to fundraise for the Christchurch massacre victims. This was at the end of February 2020.

Rick's good friend Ronald in Tauranga, New Zealand had told him that his daughter-in-law was a doctor in Christchurch and had volunteered to help with the recovery of bodies and help medically with the severely injured. She had told him it was like a war zone. A military-style semi-automatic weapon can mutilate a person's body, ripping organs and limbs to shreds.

With the Covid thing happening, Victoria would do the run but would have to scramble to get on one of the last flights out of Auckland into Australia before New Zealand's borders would close for total lockdown.

Arriving back in Australia, Victoria faced a two-week mandatory isolation. Luckily, Rick and Victoria had a unit in a hotel complex that was satisfactory for the police, who were monitoring every flight coming into the country.

Quarantine otherwise would be in designated hotels for the two weeks.

Australia, one of many countries in complete lockdown.

Rick had also left a few days before to work in Western Australia (WA). Then the WA state government and the Queensland state government—along with Victoria, NSW, South Australia, Tasmania, and Northern Territory—shut their borders. Rick was trapped between borders with hundreds of other fly-in fly-out workers. He would not be able to get home for another five months.

You could say he was stateless.

It didn't stop Rick taking his remote controls and radio monitoring systems with him.

Meanwhile other businesses were collapsing due to the lockdown.

People and families were losing hope. It was a no-brainer, you lock people inside for weeks at a time, they begin to lose hope.

The worst affected with the spread of the virus was Victoria, NSW, and South Australia. There were cruise ships that were mooring off the coast of NSW and WA with infected people needing medical attention. The crew was told not to bring sick people ashore but they had no choice but to do just that. No ship was allowed to berth at these ports but had to remain off shore.

Rick played the stranded tradesmen flying in and out of Perth up to the Pilbara with the mining company when work was available. Sometimes he would be on a night shift for ten nights straight for twelve hours and be off for two weeks. This gave him time to keep the plan together and make sure everyone was sticking to the plan.

A Beach Baron light twin aircraft was hangered in a farm shed just out of Mount Isa, Northwest Queensland, and only Foxtrot and Alpha (Rick) were able to fly it under radar, with transponder turned off, so no GPS tracking could monitor their position. And no flight plan would be filed interstate.

Foxtrot had agreed to carefully be disguised as a stranded back-packer from South Queensland to get on a bus with a new identity and travel to Mount Isa, where he would be picked up by a farmer who supported the group. Once arriving, Foxtrot would immediately use an old cell phone that had no GPS tracker on it and ring Alpha to give him an update on the plane and where he was to fly, using the aircraft as a VHF transmitter point in sky covering a range of kilometres. He also would discard the cell phone so that no trace by police from any cell towers in the area could give their position.

All radio communication on the ground and in the air would be kept to a minimum and Foxtrot would fly outside the Brisbane radar and Melbourne radar coverage, in their blind spots with the transmitter. Foxtrot would cover the registration of the aircraft. Only the farmer would know these details and he was a very reliable source, as Alpha (Rick) had helped him many times with electrical and mechanical aid when his farm was suffering the severity of the Queensland droughts.

Rick had learnt this idea from a CIA secret airline that never officially existed, "Air America," which operated in Laos during the Vietnam War by using aircraft to fly up to the highest mountain terrain and become a VHF transmitter for personnel on the ground on the other side of the terrain.

Foxtrot would arrive on a Brisbane to Darwin bus in Mount Isa in the early hours of a Tuesday morning in late March. He had been stood down by Qantas as a junior first officer on Airbus A330s by this time, and Alpha (Rick) and Foxtrot had discussed plans in Brisbane in early January what they would do if this virus situation spread.

So, having set up the operation hub in an old warehouse for Alpha, Foxtrot (Elton) was ready to fly some hours in circles as a VHF transmitter covering a number of kilometres around the state of Australia and then secretly hide the Beach Baron back in the old hanger under wraps.

Old wartime radio equipment would be used as no interceptors would be able understand how equipment seventy-five years old operated. Alpha had thought of everything.

Delta (Jimmy) was busy covering his identity in the team with his engineering business. He knew many people in state government and was able to get information about the Premier's next moves.

Foxtrot would continue flying each day, depending on the weather, for up to six hours. There were also provisions for another pilot to come and relieve him after a four-day period and Foxtrot would continue being busy with the communication network.

With the plan, the whole concept was to get as many people working in an undercover environment without any trace for the police or military finding them or their equipment.

There was also another purpose for going under cover. A stage two plan was going to take place which had incorporated collecting printing plates off an underground market over a number of years, not just any printing plates but overseas government printing plates, U.S. $100 note printing plates.

Alpha reckoned if a government can print notes out of nothing and claim it's legal tender for the populace and charge interest on it as it devalues and as the banks do on numbers they make up, it's not fraud to do the same thing with authenticated printing using government printing plates and legitimate serial numbers on each $100 bill.

The three things you need to print the bills:

1) Plates
2) Authenticated paper. It had to be genuine.

3) The ink or dye.

They would have a machine set up as well to haul the dry notes into new bundles of $100 bills.

Rick had thought about the Australian $100 note, but didn't know where to start, as most Australian notes of all amounts had windows in them and he didn't have the paper or plates to copy.

Over the last ten years, Rick had purchased thousands of U.S. $1 dollar bills and knew he could clean them down to nothing with a very special cleaner and reproduce them as $100 bills with the authenticated serial numbers on as mentioned. He had kept this to himself over those last ten years, as he had bought U.S. currency when he had travelled to the U.S. for family visits. He would purchase from cities, counties, anywhere where he could lay his hands on it, quietly bag them up tight in concealed clothing boxes, and ship them back to Australia.

Now with the underground movement, which was growing to a sizeable number and a qualified printer who had lost his job previously, they were in business.

Lima, with three of his trusted men, would embrace and protect the safe houses with automatic pop-up cameras, camouflaged pit holes around the properties, and secured and concealed automated doors with cameras on all angles inside and outside that were not visible at a distance. Cameras were connected to monitors in a safe or panic room down in a concrete basement in each house.

The houses themselves were a little rundown so as not to attract any attention. Some had been bank mortgage sales bought with a small amount of cash.

The only defensible weapon Lima carried these days was a taser.

Over the last six years, Alpha (Rick) had been flying from the east to west coast of Australia, depending where companies wanted to position him for his expertise in the electrical engineering side. Rick wasn't a full Electrical Engineer, but he had the technical knowledge and experience most engineers would not have and he used it to his advantage.

He flew up to the Pilbara and Port Hedland, to the iron ore shipping port maintenance shutdowns for BHP and Roy Hill mining operations. The iron ore ships were still coming in numbers, up to fifteen could be counted off the west coast moored in the Indian Ocean. As one ship was piloted out, another ship would be piloted in to berth at the BHP, RIO TINTO, FMG, ROY HILL and a few other berthed for copper, zinc, and salt.

A helicopter would be flying day and night, taking the pilot out to the ships, and when the ships came into the harbour, they would be literally twenty-five centimetres off the bottom of the ocean floor. Within seventy-two hours, they would be loaded up with 180,000 tons of iron ore or more and sail on the tide, which would have risen by twenty metres. Three tug boats would help guide a super iron ore ship out.

Rick would help look after the maintenance at the port or inland on the mine sites with his other trade colleagues, not knowing everything Rick had and was setting up. Once arriving back to camp, a quick shower, dinner and then he'd get on his monitors and in contact with the team.

Charlie (Paul) was organising an old car (Holden utility) to pick up the bags of clothes with Tango (Georgia). They had disguised themselves as a little old couple taking bags of rags and old clothes to the second-hand clothing stores. These bags were full of U.S. $1 notes.

Charlie and Tango were able to move around the checkpoints, as no one would suspect a little old couple in a rundown old car taking bags of old clothing to a second-hand store. They even made sure they were not in full focus of overhead cameras.

There were police checkpoints everywhere from Mackay to every main city to provincial areas and even on the outskirts of country towns, to ensure people were not crossing borders illegally and were following lockdown procedures to stop spreading this virus.

Sadly, you always get a number of people who don't care about anyone except themselves and ruin things for everyone else. This could be seen on the beaches, with partygoers, and collective groups. This helped spread the virus.

Inside the police operations room in Brisbane, the camera and microphone planted inside the wall lining by Tango (Georgia) near the main operations hub, looking straight above the desks, was doing its job discreetly.

Rick could hear and see everything going on in that room thousands of kilometres away, and no one would know who and where the brains of the operation was. He could hear the senior officers talking amongst themselves about how to catch a rogue operator who had taken a number of people with their businesses and employees and simply disappeared. The police were trying to trace where the currencies from a number of banks were disappearing to in small foreign bills. It was depleting the banks' overseas trading currencies as the banks unscrupulously used these to make millions of dollars in a short space of time.

Meanwhile, Michelle was designing escape tunnels between three safe houses and the printing mint.

These were dug carefully with small machinery so as not attract attention by those listening out on noise monitors that would pick up vibrations indicating the area where the noise or noises were coming from.

As soon as the $1 U.S. bills were cleaned and placed in the $100 plates in the press with the required dye, the printing machine would extract them in a dry state and pack them in bundles of a thousand, then place them in plastic bags in perfect and identifiable U.S. government condition. These would have the correct serial numbers on each bill, according to the plates.

The next stage of the game would be to release these bills to buy very carefully from every gold and silver supplier around Australia and on the overseas market, without the market being flooded with U.S. currency or creating suspicion for the police or government authorities picking up the trail quickly.

Eventually the police would be on the trail, but the team was always one step ahead and knew in advance what they were going to do.

Every able person in the underground movement would be transported in groups of five in a central area such as Mackay and smaller provincial townships where banks were few in number. But in cities such as Brisbane, Sydney, Melbourne, Adelaide, Perth, Darwin, and Townsville, they would go in groups of ten.

Each person dressed as a professional person, and would be representatives of frontal companies going to designated gold and silver buyers and sellers at allocated times. Purchases would be made in cash with no receipts.

Transport to and from these areas would be by plane, bus, and cars set aside by Charlie as well as trains. For any public transport, they paid in cash; otherwise, if cash wasn't accepted, they would use certified bank cards that could only be traced back to European banks.

The idea was to buy back as much gold and silver and shares in precious metals to offset what the banks had burdened people with in debts and financial hardships over the years.

"And we aim to please."

Trading in pure gold stocks as it was increasing in value on a daily basis and buying back fifty tonnes of gold and silver meant printing a lot of currency. The printing press and the cleaning down of thousands of $1 bills meant the press would be printing day and night. And quietly, the ongoing buying of $1 U.S. bills would be from NZ as many of Alpha's (Rick's) friends had collected them over the years for travel, collecting from the private sector (as word got around and what it was for). Small neighbouring countries such as Singapore, Thailand, Vietnam and a few others were all contributing under certain conditions. Alpha had taken his time over the years to plan every detail and look at every possibility of what could go wrong.

When people are offered an incentive, money talks and $1 U.S. bills did not seem like much to dispose of to many influential persons in these countries.

How Alpha got these bills to the printing press was a mystery to most. All they knew was that bags of rags and lots of rags could only come in by ship from these Asian countries, as their airlines had stopped flying. The bags of rags were the key.

Alpha only confided this part of the operation to those running the command post and leading.

The race, training and minting currency, was on. The teams would not leave till everything was in order. The police were confused as there was no paper trail and no fingerprints on anything including cars, motorcycles, papers, books, and bills handed over. Alpha could see and hear everything happening and conversations in the police command centre from Western Australia and Queensland. The police realised their only hope was to make contact with the brains behind the organisation.

The team of people were increasing in every city and province in Australia initially, and then throughout the cities. People were literally going off the radar. They held no bank accounts, and had no household or utility bills that could be traced.

The team knew they could rely on each other and best of all there were no crowded spaces, no outside control, no manipulation from the outside world.

A plan had been implemented on food supplies over the years and already manufacturing and food suppliers had become undercover agents for Alpha. Although many had never met Alpha, he helped them maintain their businesses. At this moment in time with Covid 19, it came as a blessing to them and their families and they remained loyal to the program.

Meanwhile Alpha (Rick) was enjoying classical music, which gave him so much inspiration, even in times of uncertainty. He had played his cornet with orchestras, trumpet concertos, and with brass bands on tours over the years and longed to be able to play out again instead of having to work so hard. At that very moment whilst Alpha was in his trance, the news came that the borders between Queensland and Western Australia would close at midnight.

Now Alpha was trapped between borders. Queensland had closed its borders and, where Alpha was working, Western Australia had closed its borders also due to the strain of the Covid virus. Things were becoming very uncertain for everyone not only in Australia but the world in general. People would be under lockdown in their own homes as well as being stood down from their jobs. The financial burden would be on households and then there would be pressure on state and federal governments to do something.

Alpha's wife Victoria managed to catch the last flight with Air New Zealand from Auckland to Brisbane and then to Mackay, entering Queensland. She would have to now go into fourteen days of self-isolation. This would test Victoria's ingenuity.

Working away from his family was not a good thing and he knew that now. Alpha would not realise it but he wouldn't see his wife and family for another five months, till he could get home again.

TIME TO PLACE STAGE TWO INTO OPERATION

The currency heist had begun. The teams would leave from different venues. The U.S. $100 bills would be placed in gold and silver buyers' hands very discreetly. No receipts.

This also gave Alpha hope along with other friends and families. You cannot buy back time but you can make it a priority to have finance behind you to give you time.

Meanwhile the police in Brisbane, Mackay, Rockhampton, Cairns, Townsville, and Gladstone were using a number of police resources, going door to door, asking people if they knew of the team's whereabouts as they had simply vanished. The police had no leads.

Bank accounts had not been used, household accounts had not been touched, children had not been seen.

The team hadn't vanished, it was just they were using their resources in a different way and they were not being controlled by a system.

"Who is this Alpha?" the police superintendent, Jim Collins, was asking. "Get me every resource that identifies this person, I want to know where he works, what he does, fingerprints, what state in Australia he lives in. I want a picture and some fingerprints now!"

Meanwhile Alpha (Rick) was dancing around his chair in his makeshift control room in WA. Lima (Brian) was operating out of the command centre out of Mackay. He was dancing too. These centres were untraceable. The police had no leads to go on, no actual physical person to put a picture to a name and no fingerprints.

"This guy is invisible," the Chief Superintendent was yelling, "and we cannot find any law he has broken."

"But we are losing communities and we still have to deal with Covid and lockdown," another senior officer was saying.

The question remained: "How are these communities living?"

In Alpha and Lima's minds, "If people lived under liberty and free enterprise as they should be able to live, the world would be a happier and contented place."

Not socialism, communism, nationalist socialism, or globalism, all of which destroys the soul and under which the majority is controlled by the few.

Alpha was playing his aces.

"If you're going to play the game, boy, you gotta learn to play it right."

Alpha was playing it right. The police were playing right into their hands and the powers above from state premiers to legislators wanted answers.

Meanwhile the communities of people from all walks of life were driving, flying, busing, walking, biking, all discreetly and spread out over different states, using their U.S. government minted notes to buy precious metals in small and medium amounts to not attract suspicion.

Of course, there would be the few dressed up businessmen who would be making great accolades on how they wanted to back their businesses financially by purchasing bars of gold for special and safe storage, with no questions asked from the gold dealers.

After the charade, every vehicle was wiped clean and parked up. Bus tickets, airline tickets, bank cards, and anything with fingerprints was destroyed by chemicals or fire. No tracers whatsoever.

Tango (Georgia) had made and was making perfect disguise features for everyone in the area of Queensland, in between her police station cleaning job. Also, she discreetly overheard and reported police conversations. Other states had operatives trained to do the same job.

It was becoming successful with the field operatives. But just to stop nosy gold dealers asking questions, no one person would ever purchase twice from the same dealer.

Of course, Alpha's Asian friends were quick to accept the $100 U.S. dollar bills, as they saw it as a strong base, but Alpha knew currency was starting to break down. He never let on why he wanted the precious metals in exchange and they never asked.

Government law says you have to declare everything when selling precious metals over $5000, but it doesn't say anything about reporting when purchasing.

Alpha's aim was to aggressively purchase and store up to fifty tons of precious metals in specified hidden locations. These would be distributed evenly when the time came.

This was bargaining power when a crooked system collapses for the communities that had taken the initiatives to see themselves saved from the hardships to come.

> **DON'T WORRY ABOUT PEOPLE GOD**
> **REMOVED FROM YOUR LIFE.**
> **HE HEARD CONVERSATIONS YOU DIDN'T,**
> **SAW THINGS YOU COULDN'T, AND**
> **MADE MOVES YOU WOULDN'T.**

Romeo (Graeme) was still in Turkey purchasing more precious metal to be shipped to Australia. He wouldn't leave till all the consignment was together, there were no loose ends, shipping charges and customs had been paid for a second time and his air ticket back to Australia was confirmed.

Romeo had purchased considerable extra amounts of precious metals in the six months he had been stranded there under lockdown, and was able to have finances channelled to him through various parts of the organisation. But he was starting to get a little tired of being in an Arab country not knowing very many people, under lockdown, and with very cold temperatures.

Once again, everything had been purchased in U.S. currency. The only criteria now would be how he got it through Australian customs. As this consignment was coming under a separate business operation, it would have to be declared. Again, this would be declared as a purchase not a sale, so all expenses paid out for the inconvenience of having to stay in Istanbul could be claimed against taxes in Australia.

Alpha was making sure every angle had been covered. The police had no idea about this operation nationally or internationally, all they were aware about was dissolving communities. By the time questions about the amounts of U.S. $100 bills being cashed in to banks around the country and overseas and questions were asked, by the time there was police involvement checking for counterfeit or fraud, Alpha and his team would be well on their way to completing stage 3.

By the way, the money was not counterfeit, it was backed by the U.S. government. It just hadn't been commissioned by the U.S. government.

YOU'D BE SURPRISED WHO IS WATCHING YOUR JOURNEY AND BEING INSPIRED BY IT. DON'T QUIT.

Meanwhile the printing press kept running. Authenticated $100 bills were being produced and there were a lot of U.S. dollars cashed in at banks around the country from businesses, especially precious metal merchants.

The government was increasingly putting pressure on banks to check and scrutinise personnel and business accounts for money laundering or to prevent money being transferred to terrorist groups or so they were saying. People were having to sign documents and give personal details of where they worked and lived at every bank. This had to be a breach of privacy as when you open account at any bank, don't you always fill in those details then?

Even sending currency through to Romeo in U.S. dollars, a bank had blocked an account to stop the transfer, stating the money was going to a scam. This put pressure on the owners' accounts not being able to transfer money for everyday expenses.

Romeo was still having to make sure his sister's medical expenses for necessary operations were covered. There was ongoing rehabilitation to strengthen the bones and muscles and keep her mental health intact. No person had been caught for the hit and run that nearly left her dead.

They were living in a society where many people do not want to take responsibility for their actions and are willing to blame society for their circumstances is not acceptable.

Even Delta was running out of patience with those who were flouting the law in regard to those who were not accepting medical advice to protect themselves and others against Covid19.

Beach parties and social gatherings with infected people was only a glimpse of what was yet to come.

The military had been called to coordinate with the police checkpoints on borders, airports, roads, and public places to make sure people were doing the right thing. Businesses were closed, with retail, hospitality, and tourism businesses suffering the most.

Meanwhile Alpha, Lima, and Delta were coordinating the next phase of operation to confuse the authorities. Teams of persons all over were still continuing to purchase precious metals and the Asian supplies of rag containers were still making their way through customs.

Foxtrot had infiltrated customs computers to annul any suspicion on certain consignments and remove any camera footage of these consignment boxes. Foxtrot was able to do this by hacking into the national database for Australian customs. This had carefully been done in advance of the operation.

Alpha, from his makeshift office down in the basement of Delta's (Jimmy) apartments in Perth, was waiting for the police to catch on to the money trade. Which they did. The amount of U.S. $100 bills had saturated the CBA, NAB, ANZ, Bendigo Bank, not so much the smaller banks as they were community based and these weren't the main target banks in Alpha's portfolio of banks.

Alpha's plan wasn't to steal currency or overinflate it with numbers and figures at high interest rates but print it and give it back at competitive rates and purchase proper money (gold and silver) to bring a real value to those who had been penalised over the years for their hard labour and loss of earnings by the elite.

The last stage of the plan would follow later on when the U.S. $100 bill plates would be sent back to the U.S. Federal Reserve with a thank you note, leaving the Federal Reserve in a compromised situation. However, Alpha wasn't there yet.

The State Police and Federal Police were called in to study all the camera footage and amounts of registered U.S. $100 notes. These weren't counterfeit, they were genuine with registered numbers. People were bringing them in from all over Australia and could not be identified. This was part of the training Alpha and Delta had installed into each field person, to never disclose a face to the cameras in the bank. "Always have a head down and never disclose any body feature or markings to identify your person, but be fully polite."

Alpha and Tango had studied every bank layout, every angle, every camera possible in the last eighteen months. And although most if not all the field operatives were dealing with gold merchants, there were times when only Australian currency was accepted. So currency had to be exchanged.

The police superintendent Jim Collins and his team were beginning to lose a lot of sleep over this whole situation. This wasn't now just a state situation, this was a federal situation.

They needed the best forensic experts to find something, a hair, a fingerprint, a photo, or possibly to track a phone call. "We need a communication line with these people," Jim screamed. "They know we are on to their money laundering scheme."

Effectively it wasn't money laundering. It was printing currency with official U.S. government plates and giving it back to the banks with no interest charged, not the other way round, printing money and creating numbers with interest.

The only law that had been broken was having official govern-ment printing plates and printing more numbers than the federal reserve could handle.

When this scheme couldn't be contained, it was eventually leaked to the public. The press had a field day and this was adding to the strain of the government agencies. They had been outwitted by some so-called amateurs, as Jim Collins would like to call it. But he couldn't understand the motive. Jimmy Collins had been work-ing in a misguided system, a policing system that was broken with corruption and legal interference. He was blinded by all this as this was why he could not see the Alpha team's motive.

They, Alpha and team, only had to make one slip, one person who could identify them.

The transmitter in the operations room was working very ef-fectively. The conversations were very intense amongst the police ranks. The sound and phone analysts' team in the centre were trying to intercept phone calls from any cell phone calls passing messages or conversations between the group.

Then came the one phone call between a nurse and Zulu (Michelle) the tunnel architect. It was a quick call about a patient that needed some medical attention from an infection and she would have to use the south tunnel to get the patient out for treatment.

Zulu was taken by surprise as phone calls could only be made on old cell phones with no GPS tracking devices. The phone call was short, but was just enough time for the authorities to find the cell phone tower in the vicinity where the call was made.

The patient was taken down through the south tunnel quickly, whilst the police were placing into position as many personnel as possible to narrow down the search.

Arriving at the tunnel entrance and quickly getting out with the patient, the nurse and helper quickly sealed off the entrance from around the safe house.

As they were moving around in the darkness and onto the street, a police vehicle intercepted them and asked what they were doing. Initially, they were taken into custody. The person needing hospital attention was quickly seen by a doctor and would remain in hospital for a few days under police supervision.

The nurse and company were detained and then taken to the police headquarters at Brisbane central police station.

Tango had been in the operation centre that morning and recognised the nurse in police custody. The nurse caught a glimpse of Tango and carefully gave a signal with her fingers, scratching her head that nothing would be revealed.

The microphone and monitors that were being carefully watched and listened to in the panic room, with the information Tango had picked up on the nurse, were being carefully scrutinised by Lima and Alpha through a patch in to his room at camp at Port Hedland. Delta, Foxtrot, Charlie, Tango, and Romeo would also be briefed.

Every safe house and living facility had its own coordinator to coordinate resources for every day issues. This would only be for a time as families would eventually be able to re-establish themselves and exist on a new financial plan.

It was time to make contact with this inspector Jimmy Collins and get the nurse and patient back.

Alpha, as part of stage four, would initiate a phone call under a disguised voice. But the transmission would come from very old military radio equipment, a signal not many people in this day and age would be familiar with, except international ham operators, and they were a dying breed.

Many of these men and women had a code they held between themselves and would not disclose information anyway. This would frustrate the authorities even more.

An untraceable phone number on a landline was made to a

designated phone line in the police operations room. Remember, Alpha is way up in the northern part of Western Australia with a two-hour time difference between WA and Queensland. Lima would be listening in on the conversation.

Alpha rang from a soundproof area. He had just got off day shift and it was early evening.

The phone rang in the police control centre in Brisbane, a line patched in to the federal police in Sydney.

"Superintendent, it's for you, it's HIM on the phone."

"Who?"

"Alpha."

"Give me the phone. Alpha, is that you?"

"Good evening, Superintendent, so nice to finally talk to you. I see you are holding one of my colleagues who was doing her job."

"Yes, she is being treated well."

"And what about you, Superintendent, are you being treated well? How's your wife and family, Superintendent? Are they seeing much of you?"

"I get to see them, but would see them more if you and your colleagues gave yourself up, Alpha. Alpha, we are on to your game."

"Superintendent, what game would that be?"

"Alpha, you're creating your own U.S. $100 bills and distributing in batches of $10,000, which is illegal. What are you planning to do with the proceeds, Alpha? And where are the communities of people?"

"Superintendent, let me remind you we have on loan U.S. $100 printing plates and their own authenticated paper to print on. There is no counterfeit in that, and even the serial numbers are authentic. You'll never be able to disprove these bills, Inspector, and the banks will have to accept them. Superintendent, do they pay you well for the hours you work?"

"Alpha, why do you ask?"

"Superintendent, you live in a system that steals from you and your family."

"Alpha, are you trying to be a Robinhood? Steal from the rich and give to the poor?"

"Superintendent, we are trying to give everybody in my trust an even playing ground. Liberty, free market. I'm not sure if you are familiar with those terms. I know you live in the environment of corruption and dominant control by the few. Let me also remind you, Robert of Loxley was a nobleman in his time who was stripped of his title for seeing injustice done to his fellow man and doing something about it."

"So Alpha, you think you are a modern-day Robinhood? Alpha, what do you want?"

"Superintendent, for a start, I want the nurse and her patient back."

"What do we get in return?"

"Superintendent, that's up to you. The only law we can be prosecuted for is printing of foreign government currency. Superintendent, don't you think the banks do even worse? They create currency that doesn't even exist and flog interest on it? To me, that's fraud. Isn't that to you, Superintendent? If you and I did that, we would both be in trouble. Good day, Superintendent."

"Alpha, wait."

But it was too late. Alpha had hung up.

"Did anybody get a fixed location?"

"Superintendent, you're not going to believe this but the signal is coming from way up in the air and bounced off radio transmssion devices all over Australia. It's technology I'm not familiar with. They have had this planned out for some considerable time."

"Keep working on it, son. This is like trying to break the enigma code from the Germans and Japanese from World War II."

A thought came to Jimmy. "Old technology."

"I want every flight plan that has been lodged with Airways Australia for the whole of Australia in the last month."

"Superintendent, that will take days as there so many scheduled and non-scheduled flights through and around Australia."

"They must be transmitting from an aircraft. How long can a light aircraft stay in the sky without refuelling and how high and what's its ceiling?"

Alpha had trained everyone on his team about dealing with the opposition. When they think they are on to you, change tactics.

Superintendent Jimmy Collins was grasping at straws. He was thinking about old technology but he was sure it would never work from his opponent's side. Trying to understand how Alpha knew so much about their moves in the operation centre, Jimmy was becoming a bit paranoid and thought there was a mole. He cleared everyone out except detectives Ryan and Jack and the analysts and cryptologists.

That meant Tango's cleaning ears would be gone.

The chip was still imbedded in a secure place though.

Alpha was now flying every second week up to the Pilbara, a two-hour flight north of Perth.

Foxtrot was still doing his flying thing and computer footage of all police and federal agencies as required. Who would have thought a professional airline pilot would have jumped at this opportunity, while his executive boss was still being paid his millions and at the same time standing down twenty thousand of his own employees?

The federal police were now involved with forensics. Alpha knew exactly what Jimmy the superintendent was going to do.

Foxtrot had been notified that there would be an investigation of all registered aircraft and flight plans lodged in the last two weeks, initially in Queensland and then beyond. The Beach Baron was secure but the registration was still valid, registered to Bryce Allen, owner and manager of Lockheed Station, North Queensland. It would evidently take a few days to investigate where the Beach Baron was located and unless they were flown in, it was a long drive from Mt. Isa to the station. The police would be using up a lot of time and resources on a hunch that would be right, but Alpha and the team were one step ahead. When you use the opposition's resources to chase you on a hunch, eventually they are going to be drained. They would rely on the public giving information at a cost or reward. Have you ever heard of a reward being given out?

Foxtrot knew all of North Queensland and the Northern Territory. He would fly the Baron up to Darwin for maintenance. He would lodge a flight plan from Darwin to Broome and then cancel the flight as if to land at a station nearby. This would give him cover and time to reposition his moves with the generosity of the grazier that knew Foxtrot and his family.

Meanwhile Zulu had a good team together in the Brisbane area. They were building more good-sized tunnels between safe houses. These would replenish food supplies, water, and every possible need for families in safe areas. Home schooling was also a priority. The spoils from the gold merchants were carefully placed in locations only the team members were given access to. This was to prevent any discourse on who was entitled to what.

Tango kept up the disguises. Jimmy, over on the west coast, was the ears and the eyes on the political scene as well as providing a safe house for Alpha.

Charlie maintained all the transport and the supplies they placed at allocated areas. Those older vehicles not used were disposed of.

Romeo now was waiting patiently for his flight home from Istanbul, Turkey.

There was a dead line to have the plan completed but this would just depend on the authorities and how long they wanted to drag this out. They were playing on hunches. Alpha was playing to plan. A plan that played around Covid, a plan that was going to give people their dignity back.

When you play a game of chess, you play your opposition's hand. You have to narrow down the moves or he will reverse play you till you are pinned in that corner checkmated, no place to run.

The time was ticking and that's what Alpha needed to keep strategising.

The gambling man would say he'd learned how to read people's faces so he knew what they were betting, and why, based on the way they looked at the cards and at the people around them.

Alpha's wife Victoria was in Mackay, one of the front persons with Renae close by. No one would ever suspect one of the brains behind the operation was a sweet lady who was running marathons, participating in community events, working with families and generally giving her love and attention not only to her family but those who were hurting from life's challenges as well.

All Alpha could think about was getting home to Mackay, Queensland without having to go into quarantine in Queensland for fourteen days and having to come back into WA in quarantine for fourteen days at a cost of three thousand dollars either way.

Alpha had seen the strains on people being locked down in Perth. They were going mental, losing hope. Overseas students could not get home or manage the cost of accommodation, although some could manage. Alpha's Japanese friend Teko was a blessing, he was good company and took the time to share meals with him when in Perth.

Also Big Simon, Alpha's roommate for those months, was a blessing; he was there for Alpha and always gave a word of encouragement when Rick was feeling the strains of this virus in the community. The streets of Perth were empty for weeks. The airport was deserted, no planes flying. Like most other cities around Australia and around the world, it was a scary and hopeless sight.

But Alpha learnt from all of this and part of the planning for this heist came through his down time.

WHEN THE VISION IS CLEAR, THE STRATEGY IS EASY

Alpha's communication network set up by Foxtrot worked impressively. Alpha would never ask Foxtrot to hack into any network system unless it was for a good reason. There was a code of conduct which the team lived by and this mutual respect they had for each other bonded them.

Back in the command centre, every filed flight plan was coming through from Airways Australia. Jack and Ryan were going through every flight plan lodged up and down the country within the last two weeks. They spent hours combing through scanned documents and found nothing.

Jack and Ryan went through aircraft registrations in Queensland, Northern Territory primarily and then WA, NSW, Victoria. There had to be an aircraft in Northwest Queensland, again it was a hunch.

"Ryan, get me Alpha on the phone." The phone rang to Alpha's line. It was patched in by Foxtrot to Western Australia. It was 8:00 p.m. Western Australian time. Alpha usually monitored his phone from 5.00 a.m. to 8:00 p.m.

"Superintendent, how are you today?" said Alpha. "I hope you are not under too much stress."

"Stress, what do you know about stress? I have the Premier on my case, the Federal Police Commissioner asking me what's going on, and to top it off, the Secretary of State from the USA is asking me how on earth did these thieves get those $100 bill plates, paper, and dyes? The Federal Reserve has gone ballistic on recovering those plates. Alpha, how did you get those plates? Or, what's your real name? Bruce, Jack, George? I'm just talking to a letter in a phonetic alphabet."

"Superintendent, where do you buy your toothpaste to brush your teeth in the morning?"

"What, Alpha? I'm asking you about plates and you're asking me about toothpaste for brushing my teeth. What is this, a soap opera?"

"Superintendent, the same reason you buy toothpaste from your preferred shop is the same reason I acquired those plates from a preferred seller. We only mean to borrow them for a time and then they will be sent back to their rightful owner."

"Jack, what does he mean by that?"

"The place he acquired them from was seller's market. You can buy things at the right price."

"Jack, you and Ryan check out every dealer, buyer, seller, runner, anyone who can give you names of those purchasing government mint printing plates illegally."

"Superintendent, you'll never find where those plates came from as the seller is offshore."

"Alpha, we know you are using some form of aircraft as a transmitter very high in the sky. They used the same process in Laos during the 1970's over very high terrain so the persons on the ground on the other side of mountainous terrain could keep in contact."

"Very good, Superintendent, but my pilot doesn't stay in one spot. Moving around gives him cover."

"And you're not using GPS, cell towers, or HF radios, what are you using?"

"Well, Superintendent, let's just say experience comes with age."

What did he mean by that? Jimmy Collins asked himself.

"Superintendent, are you going to release my nurse and her patient? There is nothing you can hold her with."

"You'll have to come and get her though."

"Superintendent, your men picked her up, do you not have the courtesy of dropping the nurse and her patient back at her house?"

"Very well, Alpha."

Alpha knew she had been bugged or even had an inbuilt camera on her, a chip implanted in her skin without her knowing. The best solution would be to have her taken outside the perimeters of the safe houses and to completely scan her. Lima had a noisy clapped out flat deck that would muffle any sound on any speaker.

Lima had been stuck on the eastern seaboard of Australia due to Covid and was making the most of the situation. This, apart from working on heavy mining vehicles, was a great challenge for Lima. Lima was playing security, work-ing as a machine operator, and was responsible for all the team and persons that had backed the team. He had suffered emotion-
ally from the horrors of war over recent years, but his joy and love for people as well as his leadership skills had taken away all those thoughts of unworthiness, resentment, bitterness and anger. Lima served his country but even more now he was serving others and he was thriving.

The vehicles he procured through friends and organisations was exceptional. Lima even disposed of some so no traces of fingerprints or DNA could be found. This flustered every move of the police.

Now Lima was in this flat deck truck with the nurse and patient. A deliberate loud muffled noise from the high revving of the engine gave Lima the opportunity to scan the nurse for bugs.

She certainly had been implanted with one in her neck. She must have been a little drugged as she could not remember anything about an incision. There was also a bug planted in her nurse's bag, a dead giveaway. The important one was removed from her neck and both were discarded outside.

❋

The police were also tracking the truck. Lima had planned ahead, remembering the training from Alpha. Always have a double so when you move a pawn forward on a chess board, you also play the one to remove the competition and he has to reassess his moves.

Lima had two of the same trucks. It would only take a blind corner and an exit road with the other truck travelling at the same speed and Lima's truck turning off quickly without being seen. The dummy truck would have travelled a number of miles before the police would have stopped it and found that the occupants were not the nurse, the patient, and the driver.

THE OLD DUMMY TRUCK ESCAPE

**ACTIONS PROVE WHO SOMEONE IS,
WORDS JUST PROVE WHO THEY PRETEND TO BE.**

"Superintendent, we've lost them. They played the dummy truck, it must have been on a blind corner and an access road nearby."

"Jack, did you get a vehicle registration and a look at the driver?"

"Yes, the vehicle registration we did get. The vehicle was registered to a Queensland cattle station but the vehicle itself was deregistered a year ago."

"Jack, I want you and Ryan to check every wrecking yard for any truck this size and colour being dropped there for scrap. Did you get a match or photo of the driver?"

"Yes, a partial photo we can possibly match with a databank. But again, there possibly may not be any criminal convictions against these people as they are working on their own convictions."

"What do you mean by that, Jack?"

"They believe they as a team are working for a cause."

"Jack, these people have broken the law."

"Superintendent, these people have half a nation behind them and they would probably be helped if required by them."

"Jack, you're becoming soft. You have a job to do, to uphold the law."

Jack was beginning to wonder who the bad guys were here. There was some truth in what Lima was saying about a failed corrupt system that manipulated people and stole from the very people who had voted the system or governments in.

Jack was a cop that up held his police oath, to serve and protect the public. The system hadn't bought him out, and he was ready to do the right thing even if it meant losing his badge.

Jack wasn't going soft but was recognising the facts.

Superintendent Jimmy Collins was wondering how in the heck Alpha had managed to get authenticated paper to print all those notes and what was his plan. It couldn't last, he would eventually run out of paper and dye for the print. There must be some other logic behind it. People dropping out of the system. Remember the taxes come from the working employees and not the businesses. The government needed to support big business and private enterprise to employ people. Businesses have the luxury of writing off expenses and gaining the tax advantages. Where was Jimmy Collins going with this? If we don't have tax payers, the government has to borrow more money (currency) from the world bankers with high interest. Our taxes pay the interest on the loans the governments around the world will never be able to pay down.

"Alpha's purchasing gold and silver bullion. That's what the U.S. $100 dollar bills are for."

Where is he holding all this and how much has he accumulated over the last month or more of this operation? Jimmy Collins wondered.

"Everyone gather around, they are storing gold in massive quantities. Jack and Ryan, I want you to go to every gold and silver merchant in the Queensland area, make phone calls if you have to. I'll contact the federal police for assistance in every other state. The rest of you go door-to-door in the area you found the nurse and extract information."

Jimmy remembered how the Nazis during World War II had stolen a considerable amount of gold and artefacts from the European Jews and smuggled some out to certain European banks. Those countries remained neutral and had hidden the rest in salt mines and lakes of Austria.

The difference was that Alpha and his team were not stealing gold and precious metals, they were making a down payment from stolen printing plates and purchasing it with authenticated U.S.

$100 notes. They were working on the theory of giving back to the masses of what has been rightly stolen from them through a corrupt banking system as Alpha talks about.

Why had it come to all this? A failed governing system. The citizens of Australia were looking for answers, and what was required was a strong and balanced governing body that could lead the country into prosperity and hope once again.

Jimmy Collins had spent thirty years in the Queensland Police Force and sworn an oath to uphold the law and protect Australian citizens. Jimmy had seen corruption weeded out in his own ranks and many criminals brought to justice. He had also seen the lives of a few of his colleagues lost in the line of duty, but this was still a legitimate case to bring before the justice jurisdiction of Queensland and now the Supreme Court of Australia. Was Alpha trying to be a modern day Robinhood? And who was Alpha?

"Get me Alpha on the phone again."

The phone was patched through to Alpha's line by Foxtrot. Foxtrot was being relieved from his flying duties for a time to concentrate on IT and technical aspects of the group. The Beach Baron was flown back to Darwin, the relief pilot was picked up, a flight plan was lodged and then terminated outside the controlled airspace. The Baron was then flown to another cattle station in the remote area of Northern Territory with transponder turned off.

"Good morning, Superintendent, what can we discuss today? Border closures."

"Alpha, we know you are stockpiling a considerable amount of gold and silver bullion. Where, we don't know."

"Superintendent, you guessed right, but your resources will be stretched, as Australia is a very big country."

"We have police going door-to-door where the nurse was found, Alpha."

"My guess, Superintendent, is that you will find a few empty houses that will bring you to a dead end."

"Alpha, your man that drove the flat deck truck with the nurse, we managed to get a partial face description. Brian Cowl is it, decorated soldier, distinguished in combat. He is a supervisor on stand down in the coal fields due to the Covid crisis."

"Lima was only there to pick up the nurse. You have nothing incriminating him. He served his country well, to the point he was traumatised when coming home. He was left to pick up his own pieces. It was the community around him that supported him and he was able to move on. My recommendation to you, Superintendent, is not to mess with him."

"Well, Alpha, we are closing in on you. There are huge amounts of gold and silver being bought but from different gold and silver buyer every time. We've checked to see if we can find out who is behind it. We have checked every gold and silver buyer we believe you have visited in recent times. No receipts, no ID, smart move, Alpha."

"Alpha, with that tonnage of gold, where do you intend to store it? Won't your counterparts become a little weary and think they are entitled to what they think is theirs?"

"Jack, are we any closer to finding where that transmission signal is coming from?"

"Sir, we know its further west somewhere, but there are thousands of square kilometres between Queensland, Northern Territory, and WA. Did you find any flight plans filed and registrations of any aircraft that seemed out of the ordinary?"

"Yes, we did, but we were assured by air traffic controllers in Darwin that these cattlemen were flying themselves home on both occasions."

"Jack, check them out anyway."

Alpha had been listening to all the conversations in the background. What the Superintendent didn't know was that the team were playing them.

They would file a flight plan and a termination of flight plan out of controlled airspace. This is what some cattle or grassers do nearing home. They had a registration of aircraft. Station aircraft fly interstate. As for the gold, it was hidden carefully all over Australia. To trade in gold again would be something exceptional. The global markets and domestic markets would be a lot freer.

Alpha was hearing every conversation that the operational room could muster.

"You're out of aces," he said. "And like the song says, you need to learn what to throw away and what to keep."

At times Alpha would feel a little overwhelmed with the responsibility of caring for his team and the wonderful people supporting and being part of a program. They all had taken a risk and it could backfire on all of them, but as long as he had those aces and the time he had drawn out, the closer they were to completing the plan he had rehearsed over and over again in the last few years.

Alpha was flying up and down the west coast from Perth to Port Hedland on mining charter aircraft. This would be in the four months of living in and out of Perth. Every second seat had to be empty due to Covid, and the monotonous paperwork always started with the questions:

Have you been in any Covid affected spot?

Have you been out of the country in the last fourteen days?

Do you have a sore throat?

And then he was checked by a nurse to test him for any Covid-like symptoms before getting on the plane. On the return flight back to Perth, documents had to be carried with company authorisation advising you were an essential fly-in fly-out worker and you had authorisation to travel.

Alpha had no time to feel sorry for himself. Even his work colleagues hadn't figured out he was coordinating this massive operation, using a team to pull off and outsmart his opponents with a checkmate.

Alpha and the team had time. The police and the authorities didn't, as they had limited resources. It wasn't as though the police were trying to catch a serial killer, a rapist, or gunmen on the loose.

This was a perfectly planned operation using the skills of a number of professional people to pull off a money heist where no one would get hurt.

From a legal perspective as seen by Alpha and his team, it was no different to what the central banks do every day, in fact it was closer to being legal given that the banks' cash reserves were not backed by anything.

The police were operating out of Brisbane, backed by the Federal Police in Sydney. Alpha was operating out of a makeshift office in WA, Foxtrot was operating between Queensland and Northern Territory, Lima had two panic rooms he could operate out of in Central Queensland, Zulu could operate anywhere between Queensland and New South Wales, Charlie was comfortable with his quick motorcycle get aways in Queensland, Delta was the main information provider in WA, Tango was keeping up appearances with her creative skills operating where necessary, and Romeo had the bullion to finalise the fifty tons of precious metals.

If the police had cottoned on to the whole operation, it would be a nightmare for them.

The Superintendent had drawn at straws, waiting for a slip up. He might be waiting for a long time.

Jimmy Collins knew there was

1) an eye in the sky with a transmitter. But where?
2) the team had printed U.S. $100 bills.
   He didn't know
3) where the paper, plates or ink came from.
4) where the operation was coordinated or where the safe houses and tunnels were located.
5) the actual names of the people involved or where the gold was stored.
6) how to put a name to any faces except Lima.

This had become a headache for Superintendent Jimmy Collins. And to save face he had to move fast.

"Sir, we have just come across these flight plans in Darwin,

which seem inconsis-
tent. They are filed and
terminated outside the
controlled airspace and
the plane, a Beach Baron,
was not seen after that for
days. The plane is registered in Queensland to a cattle station near
Mount Isa."

"Have you got the name of the person to whom the plane is registered, Ryan?"

"It's registered to Lockheed Station, a Beach Baron VH ROL."

"You need to get to that station. Inform the manager you're coming as the police need to see the aircraft."

Alpha had heard this conversation as did Lima. Foxtrot was
notified quickly to get the Baron back to Hampton Station near
Mount Isa. Go to plan B, pick up the second aircraft from next station, Blackwater station at Cloncurry Northwest Queensland. The
Cessna 210 was a very fast single engine aircraft, with very high
climb performance.

Foxtrot would be airborne at dawn and fly the Beach Baron back
to Lockheed station, hangar it, and ensure the manager Bryce Allen
knew the plane was back and under cover. It would be a three-
hour flight from the top of the Northern Territory to Northwest
Queensland, flying as low as possible, and no flight plan lodged.
The police aircraft wouldn't get to Lockheed Station till around
lunch time and with the Baron back in its hangar, the engines would
have cooled down and this would work as a distraction. The engine or tachometer would have registered the engine hours and the
time spent station hopping. The manager would be asked which
cattlemen had used the aircraft and why they needed his aircraft
for those few days. The manager had a good story and stuck with
it. Everything he said could be proved—the days, dates, stockman
purchasing for grassers, why the aircraft was used and not their
own. And this is what actually happened.

❖

Whilst Jack and Ryan had flown up to Lockheed Station and interviewed the manger Bryce Allen at noon that day, Foxtrot was already in the air flying outside Brisbane and Melbourne radar coverage and his VHF radio transmitter was also giving strong signals from his position.

The chess move was bringing the pawns and knights closer to the opponent's position.

Jack and Ryan wondered how these people were always one step ahead. This aircraft was certainly in the territory operating twice out of Darwin and then disappearing.

"Superintendent, we are no closer to the truth of the matter. We found the aircraft that was operating out of Darwin and in the territory, but as it left Darwin controlled airspace, it just simply disappeared along with the two so-called cattlemen on board."

"Can these cattlemen be identified? The station manager gave me the names as logged onto the flight records and we did track one of them down by phone. His story checks out."

What Jack didn't know was the phone that Foxtrot's relief pilot was using belonged to the station manager in the Northern Territory and his phone contract would be under the station's guise.

Superintendent Jimmy Collins was adamant there was a mole in operations. How could an aircraft just turn around and land back at a cattle station thousands of kilometres away at the right time, hangered with the engines cooled? The pilots themselves had been driven away by an organised vehicle before his men Jack and Ryan had flown up there in the Police Cessna Caravan.

Police resources were being wasted and he knew Alpha knew that as well.

The question remained: where was Alpha? And who was Alpha?

Meanwhile, the police were combing the area where they believed two of the safe houses were, and the nurse and patient had disappeared back into.

There were two houses in the same location but they were different streets that looked rundown and had old bank mortgage sales.

Call came into dispatch from the armed offender's team leader in the Mackay area.

"Superintendent, can you check with the ANZ and CBA BANKS about two properties that had prior mortgage sales on them? The signs seem to have been removed and there is something odd about these properties."

"Will get onto it right now. Where are the houses located and what sort of similar characteristics do they have, Commander?"

"The grounds are tidy, the neighbours don't say much. There are these little patches in sequences all over the lawn. The windows are closed and the front door seems reinforced, Superintendent."

"Commander, send in the bomb squad. There could be booby traps in those patches on the front lawn."

Meanwhile, Alpha, Lima, and Foxtrot, seeing and hearing all this, were just about wetting themselves in hysterics. Lima had dug in stench bombs. If walked on, they would let off a stink like rotten eggs, in other words, hydrogen sulphide.

Rick had been used to this gas underground. You carry a respirator down there in hard rock mines and if the gas is pungent, there are emergency rooms positioned at different levels. Everyone is trained in procedures before going underground. On the surface, the stink bombs are harmless. Jimmy was sending in his bomb squad. If the police dogs got a whiff of it, they would be turning their noses up and diving for cover.

The neighbours had seen Lima planting these and he had been quite open about telling them and about the house with a little story, previously. They themselves couldn't stop laughing as he told them how the police would play this out. Now Lima didn't want to make a mockery of the police as they were doing their job investigating what they thought was highly suspicious and incriminating activity.

"Superintendent, we are going in."

There was a bang and a yellow cloud of smoke. The bomb squad had triggered the first stink bomb. The smell was putrid.

There were another twelve stink bombs before they could get to the front door.

The next stink bomb was triggered and the next, and the next and so it went on. There were clouds of stinky smoke and the Armed Offenders Squad coughing and spluttering in between the smoke bombs.

The neighbours were laughing their heads off, not at the police but with the stink and clouds of yellow smoke. The houses were decoys, bought on behalf of those falling to a bank mortgage sale. The owners would eventually be back in them but not until Operation Gold Heist was over.

The Armed Offenders Squad made it to the front door. Seeing it heavily reinforced, they took the liberty of using a massive ramrod to break the door down.

Rick had trained the team well. When the enemy thinks they have you in their sights and are going to take you down, leave something of encouragement for them.

The Squad moved in, checking room by room, automatic weapons held high. After they passed through each room, they announced "clear." Next room "clear," and so on. It was an empty house with a note left on the table. It read, "Welcome, we have been expecting you, make yourselves at home."

"Superintendent, there's no one in the house, just a note saying welcome with a phone number attached, signed by Alpha. Superintendent, we've been had."

"Commander, the information from the banks have told us that the same person bought these properties as mortgage sales and paid cash."

"Let me guess, in U.S. currency transferred? The other house will be the same and we are not going to make a fool of our squad again."

The second house was where the tunnel entrance was, as Lima knew the police would go to the other first.

Jimmy Collins was beside himself. *They knew we would come. But how did they know? This operation room is clean or is it not?*

"Everyone out," said the Superintendent. "I want this room turned upside down and checked for any hidden cameras and microphones, and then tell me you have found something."

With microphone and bug checking device, the operations centre police team combed the whole office. Then to their amazement they found the culprit. Tucked in the lining of the wall above a shelf overlooking the operations computer was a bug with a camera. You would never have known it was there if you weren't looking.

"Superintendent, we've found something. A bug hidden in the lining of the walls above that top shelf."

"We've got them by the short and curlies now, they won't know what to do. I think it's time we gave our little friend Alpha a call."

The superintendent was scratching his head, wondering who could have put it there.

Jimmy Collins said, "I want everyone in this building rechecked."

Rick, Lima, and Foxtrot had seen this all going on and had planned for the next move already. They knew the police would draw suspicion to their own operations room eventually.

"Bravo, Superintendent," Alpha said to himself.

Alpha was waiting for the phone call. He had all the time in the world to answer calls from his counterpart Jimmy Collins and bring in the next stage of the plan.

The line to Alpha ran hot. It would take some effort and police resources to find.

"Good morning, Alpha, we have got some good news for you and especially for the operations room."

"Good morning, Superintendent, and what would that news be, Superintendent?"

"We have found the bug placed in the operation centre here. You've been monitoring our every tactical response and playing us,

Alpha. I think it's time we turned the tables around, Alpha, don't you?" With a laugh.

"Yes, I see our network has dropped out for a bit, Superintendent, but the standby network will be coming online soon."

"What, Alpha? Who are you?" He got off the line and told his people, "Get everyone in the operations centre and now the operations centre of the Federal Police in Sydney, Perth, we need the resources to track these lawbreakers down."

And somewhere in the darkness, the gambler broke even but in his final words, he found an ace that he could keep.

Alpha still had the ace, although the Superintendent would still push against the knight on Alpha's chess board.

✳

KEEPING IN THE PUBLIC VIEWING

The detection of the microphone had been found to the embarrassment of the Superintendent and his officers. The Queensland Premier and the WA Premier were asking serious questions about operations of the Police involvement into tracking down these so-called Bandits.

The Federal Government were also involved as their American counterparts were now furious about stolen U.S. $100 bill plates printing currency which they could not control as legal tender.

Alpha was reminded that the Federal Reserve is privately owned in the United States since 1913 by the few that duped the American public under unscrupulous conditions on that little island off the southern states of USA.

Also, there is no money or should Alpha say currency in the Federal Reserve; they just keep printing out notes with no base or standard behind it. Richard Nixon in his wisdom in 1971 broke the gold standard and from then on, the Fed and the banks have just been printing currency, running IOUs between every banking institution the world over. This suited the world bankers or world monetary fund so they could take control.

Australian banks, incorporated with the world bankers and under the world banking system, were thus controlled by this corrupt system.

So Alpha had made his case to the public of Australia and the world around them on broadcasts, screened television, radio, and social media. In fact, he had the public's support. The majority had no idea the currency and bank issues were happening.

This angered the authorities and the powers that be, as some of their dirty secrets were being exposed.

The so-called bandits were the monetary institutions. Alpha had currency printed and given back or sold back through gold dealers to banks at no interest charged, so that he and his whole team could buy back a proper monetary currency that had been traded for over five thousand years. God's money, gold and silver and precious metals.

So where was the robbery in that? Alpha and his team were looking to help all those people who had been financially robbed, and these people were under his team's care.

The plates would be returned in good faith. The team would remain anonymous

Foxtrot had now hacked into the police's surveillance system going back to the operations rooms. Alpha wasn't suggesting it was a good thing, but they still needed to be one step ahead.

Meanwhile, the stack of brand-new U.S. $100 bills had reached nearly a billion. Half had been paid out in precious metal purchases.

In the last ten years, Alpha could not believe his contacts in Southeast Asia and the USA had managed to accumulate so many huge bags containing U.S. $1 bills to clean down and reprint to U.S. $100 bills. The printer had worked day and night with assistance and was happy enough to do it. His family and friends were benefiting from it.

The police and the authorities were putting together another plan. Only the few in the operations centre in Brisbane, Sydney, and Perth would know about it: Operation Sting.

The Superintendent had put a reward out for $25,000,000 for knowledge of the whereabouts of a person or persons harbouring a criminal or criminals avoiding justice in this particular case. The police in their wildest dreams would never be able to afford

$25,000,000 out of their budget.

Alpha and the team had printed off nearly a billion dollars of currency. And the team's budget could buy more than what they needed.

A fact to remember, the more currency any country prints, the greater that currency devalues. This is why now the U.S. government were extremely concerned about their $100 plates.

Many people would think $25,000,000 doesn't seem bad for a reward, but three things were against them.

1) The police would never pay this out of their budget.

2) There was no known identity of the mystery Alpha or his other colleagues and their code names, with the exception of Brian Cowls, whose only guilt was driving a nurse home.

3) The more the public became aware of the corruption from white collar crime, the more they began to push for enquiries into the banking and legal systems.

There had to be a floor in Alpha's operation somewhere, a weak link. *Maybe we could place a mole in their camp,* thought Superintendent Jimmy Collins.

"Ryan, could you go undercover and show sympathy and support, even try to find out how to infiltrate Alpha's team?"

"I have just the person, Superintendent, she is not associated with the police but is employed as a cleaner, has no criminal convictions, her background checks out. Her name is Georgia. She has said she would like to help."

The gold rush was stacking up in the tunnels. Zulu (Michelle) had cleverly devised tunnels in three different locations.

At the close of WW2, the Nazis—with their stolen loot of gold and artefacts from around Europe—had hidden these treasures in salt mines, lakes, and specially designed rail tunnels in the mountains of Germany and Austria and Poland. A big percentage has never been found.

But Zulu was being true to those families on the team and the coded team members themselves, designing tunnels under certain locations that they would never forget. Landmarks in two states and one territory. No one would be forgotten.

Alpha was flying back to Perth for his ten days off. No one in his work crew would ever suspect he was the mastermind behind one of Australia's biggest gold heists ever. Technically, apart from the printing plates, it was legal as well.

To the Australian authorities, Alpha and his team were stealing from the world banks. But to Alpha and the team, they were simply retrieving money that had been stolen from the majority, the people, by the world banks.

Foxtrot meanwhile was flying a Cessna 210M single engine around in circles, still outside Brisbane and Melbourne radar control centres with the transponder off. This wouldn't be for much longer as the gold fortune was nearing its projected target (fifty tons of 999.9 pure bullion) and the value was increasing daily. Every few days, there was a little slide in value but not enough to be concerned about.

What Foxtrot didn't count on was where he was flying directly below the flight path of commercial air traffic. He should have visualised this as Foxtrot himself had flown the Airbus A330s on this flight path and this time he had been picked on Qantas Airbus radar.

Qantas were still running a limited number of flights between Darwin and Brisbane. The captain had noted there had been a light aircraft flying round in a racetrack hold outside the Brisbane and Melbourne control centres at about 15,000 feet. The C210 M was not pressurised but Foxtrot was carrying on demand oxygen with portable breathing apparatus for flying at that altitude.

Above 10,000 feet and any higher without oxygen, you run into hypoxia problems. Without oxygen and without realising it, you fall asleep and never wake up.

The captain asked Brisbane control if there had been a flight plan lodged as he was flying in a restricted height. Was there any survey work taking place? the captain also asked.

The reply came back from Brisbane control. "QF 399, we are not picking up any transponder signals from that area, maybe a grasser filming his station boundaries. He should be on an area VHF channel L 120.55."

"Thanks, Brisbane, will try to make contact with aircraft."

"QF 399 trying to make contact with unidentified light aircraft flying at an altitude of 15,000 feet in a race track hold west of Mount Isa, do you copy?"

Foxtrot had his radio on and could hear the concerned captain's voice. He knew if he broke silence, it would give him and his position away. Keeping radio silence, he descended straight away. That voice he knew too well, it was one of the senior captains he had flown with.

If Foxtrot wanted to keep his job as a first officer with Qantas, no one must know what he was doing in his down time.

Foxtrot looked at the instrument navigation chart. He realised his mistake and would have to contact Alpha straight away about repositioning the movements of the aircraft he was flying, to avoid any other confrontational radio calls with Qantas Airbuses or any other jet aircraft for that matter.

The separation between scheduled and chartered aircraft operating high level airspace can be 1000 feet between each aircraft. Other times on a clear day, Foxtrot would have another wide-bodied jet fly under the aircraft he was flying or above him. With a difference of 1000 feet, he was perfectly safe. The danger zone lies when two aircraft are tracking towards the same height from opposite directions or converging at the same height or descending down to the same. Every instruction from the controller to the pilots has to be read back perfectly so the pilots have understood the instructions.

The Federal police were concentrating on all aircraft movements in Northwest Queensland and Northern Territory for rogue traffic, keeping radio silence and known transponder (secondary radar) on aircraft turned off.

Airways Australia Brisbane centre had advised the federal police of just such an aircraft.

Foxtrot gave one last radio call on the handheld military-style radio to Alpha, telling him he had to land immediately as the authorities would have been on to Airways Australia of any interceptions of rogue aircraft in the flight path of any commercial or chartered aircraft flying or descending at those heights.

"Keep silence and land aircraft back at the station as quick as you can get out of there. We will keep moving to other aircraft further west on other cattle stations. This you won't have to do for much longer, Foxtrot. We have secured a number of old cell phones with no tracking devices, which we can throw away."

The information had just been received by Superintendent Jimmy Collins and the federal police. A police aircraft was immediately dispatched on exact GPS co-ordinates. A chopper would be flown in from the nearest Queensland Police headquarters, which was Mount Isa.

"We've got the location now. Jack, can you narrow the stations down in the area?"

"Superintendent, there are around three hundred to three hundred fifty cattle stations in that area alone."

"We got the federal police working with us as well and they will take the lead."

"We can only get few in numbers on foot. The air is going to be our best plan of attack. We can stop them flying the transmitter."

What the Superintendent didn't know was that Alpha and Foxtrot were winding down their aerial transmitter operations in North Queensland and the Territory.

Foxtrot was on the ground at Hampton Station quick smart,

packed up and ready to be transported back to Mount Isa. His backup pilot would remain in the Northern Territory on the cattle station as a sleeper on call.

By the time any police aircraft or chopper arrived, Foxtrot would be long gone, the station owner would have his aircraft safely hangered, and the engine would have cooled down. Any questions that the police asked the manager, he could quite comfortably say aircraft was checking stock at low levels around the station. The cattle stations around North Queensland can be hundreds of thousands of square kilometres.

In Central Queensland, NSW, and WA, the state and federal police were desperately trying to find these safe houses and tunnels where the equipment and amounts of gold and silver bullion were secured. Their only hope would be to have a mole infiltrate the team's network and Georgia, who had been selected by the police headquarters in Brisbane. Georgia (Tango) was now a double agent.

The microphone chip had been found in Operational Headquarters in Brisbane and now she was working undercover for the state and federal police. They didn't know she was a key member of the team and would not compromise her friends.

Forty-seven tons of gold and silver bullion had been shipped and secured in three different locations, right under the authorities' noses. Only another three tons to meet the target. This would possibly come with Romeo from Istanbul.

Alpha was back in Perth under lockdown. People were going crazy near the accommodation where he was staying. The police had arrested a foreign national for importing and selling cocaine. He was arrested right in front of Alpha, handcuffed and taken away by police detectives. There were people living there with medical conditions. Schizophrenia was one of them. A woman arguing with herself all night. Slamming doors when personalities changed.

Another fella near Alpha's control centre went on a rampage one night after having a few to many and smashed a whole room up. His girlfriend was petrified and the police were called in.

Alpha's Japanese friend had to be protected from some violent backlash from this same fella who went on a rampage.

And it gets better, a fly-in fly-out worker inciting the residence with fighting.

Imposing laws to keep people inside is not the answer.

Alpha was able to maintain his sanity by keeping in constant communication with his team. Old technology was still prevailing. From old disposable cell phones, VHF transmitters placed on very high terrain, even when the planes weren't flying, and a network of systems set up by Foxtrot. Foxtrot was not a professional hacker into networks. He only did what he had to in opening and shutting systems down without anyone finding him. His cover work was aviation and he would remain in that until he could fly no more.

Foxtrot was now hundreds of kilometres away from where he had left the single engine Cessna 210M. He was on a bus to Mackay. The police had done everything possible to find that aircraft and pilot. The station managers were not helpful and some were threatened with aiding and abetting fugitives. Sending police aircraft up to North Queensland with staff and choppers from within the area used up a considerable amount of police resources and time.

"Superintendent, we've lost both plane and pilot."

"You got to be joking."

"No, sir, it seems the more we pursue this, the more the public are unwilling to help, or they support a cause we don't know about. Alpha and his team are not a bunch of losers but professionals."

"Surely, Jack, we must be able to pick up some DNA from something they have touched."

"That's the point, sir, everything is clean and the only fingerprints we have is of the station manager's own pilot. We have already checked him out and he's clean."

Jimmy Collins was beginning to think he was dealing with a ghost squadron. The state and the federal police were beginning to use resources they didn't have. This was becoming a national hunt for a group they called fanatics that seemed in some ways wanting to take the law into their own hands and redistribute the wealth. That wasn't quite true, as that is exactly what socialism does. Alpha had worked a free market that had been manipulated by the powers that be in the world and he had spent some considerable time to plan a heist that would not be thought possible to help those who had genuinely faced financial hardship after their years of work and heavy burdens of taxes to pay debts from governments who had mismanaged funds over the years. This couldn't be, it was going over and over in his mind. These are thugs, but what major laws have they broken? They have U.S. $100 printing plates, that's a legality on its own. Any country having its printing monetary plates stolen is an international crime. But they are printing and buying what countries should be stocking up on again, bullion. The legitimate currency was being traded back to the banks. The plates themselves would be returned, or so said Alpha.

I must be going soft, thought Jimmy Collins. *I have a job to do and I'm going to do it.*

Georgia, without the police knowing it, was Tango, the woman of many disguises. They didn't need a microphone chip in the operations room at police headquarters in Brisbane now. Tango would be the mole.

First things first, Tango would advise Alpha and Lima on an old cell phone about the role she was about to play.

Once again, the police would play into Alpha and the group's hands. The persons taken out of the system were thriving on the excitement and intrigue. They were cared for very well.

"We need to get Georgia to make contact with Alpha's group now," said Jimmy Collins.

She said she may have contacts where some of the safe houses were and she will try those leads to disappear on a pretence and go undercover.

WHEN THE OPPOSITION IS PLAYING AT STRAWS, GIVE THEM SOMETHING TO CHEW ON

This was the next plan of attack Alpha had trained his team to think about. Make the police think they have stumbled on a loose end, a fragment, a DNA of someone, or a tunnel that has been dug as an escape route completely in a different direction to where the actual tunnels had been built.

PEOPLE RARELY NOTICE THINGS IN FRONT OF THEM WHEN SOMEONE IS ESCAPING.

Zulu had been a master of tunnel layouts and had studied the areas around Brisbane, Sydney and Perth where congestion of water, drainage, electrical and sewage systems were less prevalent or non-existent. She had found the areas she could use the GPS laser to position lines through rock to specified land marks outside the cities--places where no one would ever suspect a hideaway could be without a GPS or a map with bearings on it. It was like burying pirates' treasure or for that matter Nazi gold (which we don't want to hear about, given their horrendous crimes against humanity). Even pirates had a code of ethics among themselves.

The bullion wasn't to be buried away in some unknown warehouse. It was a store house for when times got really tough.

There is a biblical story in the book of Genesis about a young man who was sold into slavery by his jealous brothers. The slave traders had taken this young man to Egypt. He was sold and imprisoned for a time before the King of Egypt (the Pharaoh) was made aware of his wisdom from another imprisoned servant of the Pharaoh. The king had had a dream that no one else was able to interpret.

It went something like this:

"In my dream, I was standing on the bank of the Nile when out of the river there came up seven cows, fat and sleek, and they grazed among the reeds. After them, seven other cows came up—scrawny and very ugly and lean. I had never seen such ugly cows in all of the land of Egypt. The lean, ugly cows ate up the fat cows that came first. But even after they ate them, no one could tell that they had done so; they looked just as ugly as before. Then I woke up.

"In my dreams, I also saw seven heads of grain, full and good, growing on a single stalk. After them, seven other heads sprouted— withered and thin and scorched by the east wind. The thin heads of grain swallowed up the seven good heads of grain. No one could explain this."

Then Joseph replied, "The dreams of the Pharaoh are one and the same, God has revealed to the Pharaoh what to do about this. The seven good cows are seven years, and the seven good heads of grain are seven years. It is one and the same dream. The seven lean, ugly cows that came up afterwards are seven years and so are the seven worthless heads of the grain scorched by the east wind. They are seven years of famine. Seven years of great abundance are coming through the land of Egypt. But seven years of famine will follow them. All the abundance of Egypt will be forgotten and a famine will ravage the land."

What did the Pharaoh do? He made Joseph the second to himself in Egypt to prepare it for the seriousness of a famine.

The world has never learnt from the seriousness of the global financial crisis of 2008. The governors of the reserve banks, and the federal reserve banks, were in a state of flux and were not sure what they were going to do about it. Effectively the world was in a state of complete meltdown within seventy-two hours. Yes, a complete world depression, from the crash of the share market stocks from Wall Street, and all the other stock exchanges around the world.

So what did the reserve and federal banks do? They printed trillions of fiat currency. This didn't fix the problem, it made it worse. This is now 2021 and the world economies are on the brink of a shutdown by the enormity of this virus Covid 19. And what are they doing again? Printing and making numbers up that don't exist. The inflation and demise of a country's wealth.

The more world governments borrow from the IMF to create inflated currencies, the more a country's sovereignty is taken away from them and the governments are manipulated and dictated to by those they are indebted to.

Alpha knew there were those who would stand with him for things that were right and honourable. They would be the few in different pockets of Australia and other parts of the world that could make a difference.

Taking from those that steal and producing what these same people would hide from ninety-five percent of the world's population was a gamble.

Alpha wasn't saying he was the answer to the world's problems. He was just using some cavalier genius given to him, learning from the best over the years.

"The difference between stupidity and genius? Genius has its limits."

A rock borer with low noise levels had been used with the help of those working with the team on a steady basis, as there was a time limit to finish the project.

At the same time decoy tunnels were being built just outside and around the Brisbane, Sydney, Melbourne, and Perth main underground city infrastructure, not very long, not very deep, with a hidden entrance via one the train tunnels to dead end drop off points.

Plans had been moved around by the underground movements team, as Zulu could not be everywhere at once. Her main objective was to formulate the four best tunnels for the major cities as the major land marks would be incorporated.

Now Superintendent Jimmy Collins and George Ladin, head of the Federal Police team, had picked up word from Georgia about anonymous drilling around and near Roma Street Parklands. Rumour had it that tunnels were being developed near the police stations, the court house, and some of the banking institutions, not only in Brisbane but Sydney, Melbourne and Perth

Georgia was about to become part of the crew for one of the tunnels, as a friend had helped her go undercover. Georgia loved it. She now was the hidden microphone who could build a story for the police and let them think they were closing in on Alpha and the team. One slight problem, the police would be heading in the wrong direction.

Back in Perth, Alpha was having to coordinate from his decoded laptop that Foxtrot had set up. With the VHF transmitters in the aircraft that had been flown around in the Queensland outback having to be redirected, Alpha was relying on the limited coverage of some of the highest points of terrain both in Queensland and New South Wales.

He had a tremendous team of players who had progressively come on board. These bushmen who knew the local areas and surroundings were able to stay in the bush under cover and place valuable short-wave transmitters from certain trig points.

The GPS directions for the tunnels had been made prior to the heist and if Zulu used them now, the GPS tracker would have picked up their exact positions.

Planning well in advance has the advantage over an ill-planned opponent.

HOPE IS THE STRENGTH BY WHICH
A SHATTERED WORLD CAN EMERGE INTO THE LIGHT

Not being able to get home for all of those five months was hard on Alpha. Delta would ensure Alpha's spirits were kept up by inviting him out, making sure the final stages of the plans were kept intact, the safe houses were working effectively, and all the information that was coming from the state parliament resources and people in WA parliament were true and noteworthy.

Delta would remind Alpha that doing things most people won't do and going the extra mile that most people won't go would bring great benefits later, and secondly, it's not what you know, it's who you know that will help you achieve great benefits also.

All these things Alpha treasured, his friends, his family, even his circumstances. Being the quiet reserved person he was, he loved a challenge.

So flying in and out of Perth with his technical job as a cover, he would still make sure all the final preparation and every last detail of the plan in the heist would be in place. Many people were depending on him and he would not let them down.

The tunnel decoys had been designed in recent months, being designed to confuse the opposition, in this case the state and federal police that would take away any finding of the real tunnels that accommodated the bullion and also take people to safety.

Tango now was the eyes and ears for the police, but most importantly she was the eyes and ears for Alpha.

In the final stages of the plan, from the safe houses through the tunnels to the storage and then to the exits, a portion behind would be blown out to collapse the walls, preventing anyone ever securing passage through after. It had to look as though nothing had been tunnelled from the other side beyond that point.

The safe houses scattered in the cities again had been all mortgage sales, bought back with cash by one anonymous buyer.

Foxtrot had made it to Mackay, once again covering himself as the stranded back packer. No trace of him flying any aircraft had been made. No fingerprints, no left wrappings, nothing to identify him whatsoever. He was a ghost.

There had been another operative flyer as part of the team flying way north of Adelaide, South Australia towards Lake Eyre. This area was very remote. The pilot was also briefed to remain clear of any flight path of scheduled traffic or radar and to allow for those times when there would be scheduled traffic before commencing his race track holding position. The wartime VHF transmitters had become very effective.

WHAT YOU LISTEN TO AND WHO YOU LISTEN TO IS WHAT YOU BECOME

With great encouragement from his team, Alpha kept playing the fly-in fly-out tradesman on the west coast of Australia. Also, his classical music which he had played so frequently with orchestral and brass band accompanied on his trumpet gave him the ability to clear his mind and reflect on the good and great things in life, the food we eat, the air we breathe, the health we have, the family that supports us, a roof over our head, an attitude of thankfulness.

Alpha was a very grateful person. It reflected in his dealing with people, the care he showed to his team. He had a carefully thought-out plan in place to rescue any of his team members if they got into trouble.

With Tango now working in decoy tunnels and sending information back to the Superintendent and George Ladin from the federal police, this bought valuable time for Zulu as Zulu was now able to progress further towards completion of the four major tunnels in each city from designated safe houses to the storage areas of the bullion. These of course would be sitting under designated land marks of each city. Each tunnel was not too deep but long enough to provide escape routes outside the cities when needed.

With the lockdowns in place across Australia and the world, finance was becoming an increasing issue for many families who were already struggling, with breadwinners not being able to work for weeks at a time. Some companies made it mandatory for staff to work from home as they could, others were left without work as businesses folded. Then the on/off wearing of face masks began.

People, families, and groups were looking for alternatives to survive and get out of a system which had consumed many without them realising it. People were theoretically running towards a cliff's edge without realising it, and only a few were taking stock of the situation and doing something about it.

These very people had prepared in time before the Covid virus started.

"Jack or Ryan, have you heard anything from Georgia, and where she is tunnelling with the group?" asked Jimmy Collins, the superintendent.

"Yes, Superintendent, they are tunnel boring near Roma St in the City. Looks like they are tunnelling towards the police headquarters and a CBA bank in the area."

"Superintendent, these tunnels haven't just started in recent days. These tunnels have been well-planned in advance and I don't know how many of them there are. Another thing, Inspector, these are proper mining tunnels cut out by professionals with some gear. These people are good, Inspector."

"Where are they dumping all the extracted dirt and rock, Jack? I want you to go to every quarry, every waste dump, every new built-up subdivision in a forty-mile radius. They got to be dumping extracted earth somewhere."

Jimmy Collins was trying to understand why they were tunnel boring towards the police headquarters and CBA bank in the area, when they had printed enough cash and accumulated tons of bullion. Who knew where they were storing it? What was Alpha's objective?

CATCH ME IF YOU CAN

"Patch me through to Alpha, please someone."

A scratchy line, but the voice came through. "Superintendent, you must feel satisfaction."

"Why do you say that, Alpha?"

"Your men have been searching for our hideouts and earth-removing areas."

"Alpha, what are you planning to do with the tons of bullion accumulated?"

"Superintendent, do you not read the financial news of the world? Precious metals are used in everything we use as consumers on a daily basis. Do you have a laptop, a mobile phone, a computer, a microwave?"

"Yes."

"What components are these items made up of, Superintendent, not mentioning iron ore and coking coal for manufacturing of steel?"

"Alpha, I guess many of the components are made up of precious metals, copper, silver, gold extracts."

In the background, the superintendent is signalling to the phone tracking technicians to keep looking for any cell phone coverage or land line they can intercept.

"So Alpha, why are you and your pretty little team extracting tons of bullion from the world's resources? Are you planning to manipulate the prices of these metals when they become valuable? Is that your intention?"

"Superintendent, we are picking up some phone traffic from

Western Australia on this line."

Jimmy Collins was thinking aloud. "Western Australia, the borders are closed, how could Alpha be operating out of there? Everyone else on his team are working between North Queensland, Northern Territory, New South Wales, and now we are tracking information from South Australia, and now WA. Our resources are stretched already. This Alpha has to be a genius or someone that doesn't really exist."

Jimmy Collins did not hesitate to get George Laban from the federal police on the phone.

"George, it's Jimmy Collins here. I don't know if you have any updates tracking this Alpha, but from speaking with him on an un-secured line, we have traced a call through to western Australia and the borders are closed. He's letting us chase his operation all over the country, and he has the resources to do it. We don't, George."

"What's your strategy, George, 'cuz the U.S. Treasury and State Department won't leave us alone."

"Jimmy, we know one thing, Alpha is stranded in WA and he lives in Queensland. What does that suggest to you?"

"George, he's either an essential worker, who has been granted special papers to move around the state, or he is a fly-in fly-out worker, categorised as an essential worker. And there are thousands of them."

"Jimmy, start with the east coasters who work in WA and we will do the same through the database in WA."

It was a good thing Foxtrot had picked up some of the incoming police calls as he was able to notify Alpha quickly that the federal police and the Queensland police were going through all the fly-in fly-out workers from the east coast of Australia to Western Australia. They were looking specifically for someone. Foxtrot had to keep the lines more secure.

It wasn't an offence to listen to police radio calls on VHF Chanel's, it was by chance Foxtrot picked the communication of persons of interest working in WA from Queensland.

This Covid thing wasn't getting any better. Foxtrot was also waiting for the call in the next few months from Qantas to start his simulator refresher courses so he would be flying the Airbus A330. In the meantime, helping his friend Alpha and the team finalis their plans and helping those who had been broken by circumstances and a system to re-establish their lives was a priority. The risk was huge but if the public were able to see through cover ups and the real financial status of the world economies, most sensible people would take the advantage of planning for some not so good times ahead just like Joseph in the book of Genesis.

Getting people back to real values, looking after your neighbour, sharing when required, helping those who are less fortunate. Being grateful, having an attitude of great fullness. Standing up for what's right and not going with the crowd. Is this a hard thing to do?

All these things flooded Foxtrot's mind.

In the next five weeks, Alpha would be able to go undercover again as he wouldn't come under the fly-in fly-out personnel. He would be working South of Perth at a refinery. A ten-minute drive to work and accommodation within the area.

At the same time, Alpha was consolidating all the information about the progress of finishing the tunnels and storing the bullion. Everyone had stuck to the plan, only with a few slight hiccups. The microphone detected at police headquarters, the safe houses where the nurse and patient were located, Foxtrot transmitting directly in line with Airways Australia flight path (that was unavoidable), discovery by police of tunnels bored out.

The federal police would now be going through the air charter manifests, checking every known fly-in fly-out worker from March onwards.

Their confusion would start when they found out hundreds of fly-in fly-out professional people had been stranded for up to seven months. Some companies like BHP, RIO TINTO, FMG, ROY HILL, paid for their own employees' accommodation on their swings off in hotels across Perth.

There were other contractors from the east coast who were having to pay for accommodation at their own expense on their swings off.

The federal police with the WA police would have to try and interview two groups of people, the company staff and the contractors.

Flights were scheduled at different times of the day out of Perth airport, at the charter terminal and the main terminal. Flights to a number of sites could not be held up as there would be a backlash of time and costs to the mining companies. These companies were already under WA government rulings, as every second seat had to be empty, thus needing more charter flights than normal.

Whilst Qantas were relinquishing some of their flights due to Covid, the charter companies were doing very well.

The second problem the police were facing was the mask issue in public places. The nursing team would surround the line-up of miners ensuring their paperwork on Covid was done and then checking each person individually as fit for work.

How do they work around this? Would the police have to interview onsite after hours? Most people didn't like talking to anyone after a twelve-hour shift except friends or family, and many go off to the gym before they sit down and eat.

The police manpower was limited and the chances of catching this organised group by the day was getting slimmer and slimmer. They had the resources, while the country's financial establishment was getting weaker by the day.

Thirdly, Alpha may have been aware of all this and might not even be anywhere on these sites. As skilled as he was, he may be working or filling in time South of Perth.

The only question that could be asked of anyone would be, "Have you noticed a certain person who keeps to himself after hours and doesn't associate much with anyone?"

There could also be a number of people like that as some people on their swings on go to work, eat and sleep, then start all over again.

George Laban, leading the federal police team, was thinking, *This Alpha fella is playing a great game of chess, every move planned, and how do we beat him at his own game? Who would be the most vulnerable or weakest person on his team?*

Meanwhile Alpha was downgrading the operation from South Perth in his rented room. Alpha was on day shift.

While the Police were looking for Alpha, Tango remained the mole in the tunnel, feeding information to both sides: correct to Alpha and incorrect to the police, both tunnelling opposite directions. If Tango got caught, she would be up for Miscarriage of Justice. Getting caught was her idea of fun.

THE FINAL COUNTDOWN

THE SHOW IS NOT OVER TILL THE FAT LADY SINGS

This was the last stage of the heist. The real tunnels were near enough to completion. The hidden storage facilities at three different locations were embedded in the rock. The printing department was to close down. The currency of U.S. $100 bills had been sufficient and the plates would be discretely packaged and sent directly to the U.S. Embassy in Brisbane.

The person again shifting the plates remained anonymous.

The shipments of rag bags with gold deposits was decreasing. These shipments were running well before Covid and completely disguised. No trace, no recorded footage, Foxtrot had made sure of that. And now to get Romeo with the final shipment out of Turkey. He had suffered the most with the quarantine, the cold, the loneliness, the language barrier, being in an Arab country.

Lima was maintaining all the security around the perimeter of each safe house. Being in one panic room, he couldn't be everywhere at once. But his cameras were his eyes and ears, not only on the surface but for the tunnels as well.

Everyone mostly worked as a team outside the leadership, but there were some moans and groans as well. Some of the personnel were becoming tired of the physical activities in moving around, purchasing, being disguised, tunnelling, family's needs, and community settings.

Lima and Zulu had to keep reminding them of the compensation plan and the benefits. This here would only be for a time, but to overcome a system that controlled the masses and rise to live above it with faith, strength, and God-given determination, wasn't that something to hold onto?

Covid had literally sucked the life blood out of people and communities.

But wait, there was "hope." Out of the hopelessness, there were people and communities rising above the ashes.

When the world was watching now what Alpha and his team were doing, this inspired other groups and communities to take action too. Not in same way but to work together as teams, be creative, and not be manipulated.

Leadership and people's interests, not selfishness and greed, were the heart of the matter.

The media had been carefully covering this Gold Heist. "A group of persons buying back real money with counterfeit currency at the expense of one country's printing machine, or as they like to say, stolen plates and paper."

It was very unusual for any media, as they usually are biased, manipulating scaremongers. Covid had come at a cost to the world and its communities, but had backfired on those who had carefully instigated it.

Out of fear came great courage, faith in a higher being, conviction and determination for change and not bondage as those at the top of the food chain were trying to impose.

The human Spirit is a wonderful thing in times like these. The value of home and relationships was beginning to re-establish itself in most people's lives.

When people are oppressed, they either stand together in conviction or stand together in hatred towards the oppressors.

Alpha stood with his fellow countrymen to confuse the opposition, but there would be something he never planned on, the weakest link, Tango.

Although Tango would never compromise her standards or her friends, she was about to get caught as a conspirator and give false information to the police, but Alpha would keep true to his word to protect all his team. Part of that plan was preparing for a member of the team getting caught and the provisions of getting free. Alpha had gone to enormous lengths to create contingencies for every possible scenario of anyone getting caught, taken by surprise, even falling into an opposition trap and how to get out of it.

Not everything can go according to the law of averages, so you always must have a plan B.

The U.S. plates had been packaged up and documented as household accessories. Of course, anything packaged coming into the U.S. Embassy or any embassy for that matter is treated as suspicious, so would be scanned for anything hazardous to cause harm.

The President of the American Federal Reserve was irate to have U.S. money printing plates out of his control, as the more currency printed, the more it devalues.

THE MOLE ON THE OPPOSITION'S SIDE

Superintendent Jimmy Collins had not completely trusted Georgia as a tunnel rat, trying to rat out where and when the tunnels would take them, so he had an undercover officer unknowingly sent in with Georgia (Tango) to establish how the perimeters of the tunnels in city area and the so-called safe houses operated. Georgia was unaware of this and unwittingly made communication with Alpha with the officer Dan nearby. Pretending not to listen, he overheard Georgia talking to Alpha and Lima with those names used.

This was the breakthrough police had been waiting for, the weakest link, and she was right in front of Dan. Georgia had managed to make that phone call on an old cell phone at the tunnel entrance in an inconspicuous place, but not out of the sight of Dan. Dan had not let on but had immediately phoned the Superintendent.

"Sir, I think we have got something. It's Georgia, I think she has a connection with Alpha. She has been using an old cell phone and I overheard a conversation with her talking to him."

"Dan, don't let her know you are listening in. Just play their game. Then we will take her out when we have more consolidated information, and we know which tunnels they are using for their operations."

"Everyone, listen up, we are very near our destination with the tunnelling," came a voice from the background. It wasn't Zulu's voice, the chief architect of the tunnels, but her colleague who remained anonymous.

❈

"We are not going to break the surface at this point. I want each and every one of you to clear out everything and move back to the tunnel entrance, near the safe house and stay there. Go about your daily duties and wait," said the voice in the background again.

Dan was noting everything that was being done and ready to report in detail what he had seen and been achieved with the lay out of the tunnel and soft tip tunnel boring machines to the Superintendent.

Why the decision to stop at the point remained a mystery to Dan.

Georgia and Dan had spent a number of days fitting in the so-called Alpha team. And now they had stopped.

The noise would have been muffled by the city traffic on the surface, only the monitor, monitoring the unusual vibrations, would have picked the underground machinery movement.

Dan and Georgia would quietly move away for a period of time and report back to the Superintendent. It would be at this point in the operations centre in Brisbane that he would be asking Georgia a few questions relating to their enquiries. In other words, Dan would come out and they would take Georgia into custody.

"What's all this for, Superintendent? I helped you in ESTABLISHING a connection with Alpha and some of his teams."

"Yes, and we know you have a direct connection with Alpha as well. We now have a tunnel connected near a safe house and we have you as one of his team members, Tango."

How does he know my code name? Georgia asked herself. *Where is Dan?* Tango asked herself.

"Tango, you are in Police custody now, not a cleaner as we now know you were a fly on the wall for Alpha. What are the tunnels in the city for, Tango?"

Superintendent shoved a gun into Tango's face as an ultimate scare tactic.

"Who and where is Alpha and the rest of the team?" asked the Superintendent.

No reply.

"Tango, if we don't get some answers, we are going to charge you with conspiring to international theft of a foreign government property, money laundering, waste of police resources, and contempt as part of an organised criminal syndicate to topple this country's, and possibly other countries', financial institutions."

Dan came out, and just as Tango now suspected, he had been playing her all along and spying for the Superintendent Jimmy Collins.

"Where are the people and the gold, Tango? If you are not going to answer the questions, you are only going to make it worse for you in a court of law, Tango."

Tango lifted up her head and said, "What can you charge me with, Superintendent? You don't have any evidence. You don't even have a phone call. Nothing can be traced, Superintendent. You're only relying on a hunch after leaving the tunnel or hearsay from your loyal Dan here."

Jimmy Collins was going red in the face, he was so angry.

Tango then said, "Alpha seems to plan years ahead for every possible scenario on both sides. He seems to have a mission to benefit the majority of the population, not the few who manipulate the markets for themselves. I don't know about you but I think he might be a hero. That doesn't mean I had anything to do with him. "

Collins couldn't respond to those questions. He couldn't theoretically charge Tango with anything except conspiring to help a so-called criminal organisation, but on what evidence? On his say so, Tango had volunteered to infiltrate the Alpha line.

Now the Superintendent was one step forward and two steps backwards. Maybe he should have waited a little longer before taking Tango into custody. With one team member in Alpha's team out of action let's just say for a time, there may have to be some more strategy put into play on Alpha and Lima's behalf. This he had allowed for.

When your opponent thinks he is gaining on you, throw a curve ball in. This was a decoy tunnel, again this tunnel would become a piece of the puzzle.

Alpha had gained the trust and respect of everyone not only in his coded team but those also who had chosen to become part of the group, refusing to let a system manipulate and erode their years of hard work of achievements and accomplishments.

The plan had gone well so far. The tunnels secretly completed in various locations around the country, the gold secured safely and ready to disperse the moment it was required, the State and Federal Police in complete disarray, the public support as new reports had been exposed on the financial systems that had secretly misguided the public over the years, and the return of the U.S. $100 Bill plates .... This was the biggest surprise of the heist to the embarrassment of the country's Foreign Affairs and the U.S. State Department.

The couriers had delivered a package to the front gate of the U.S. Embassy. It was addressed directly to the U.S. Ambassador, a note attached: "Please handle with care." This got everyone's attention as it could be a bomb threat.

The security had tightened in recent months at the U.S. Embassy as there had been a bomb threat, so nothing was taken lightly. A suspicious package was scrutinised for any traces of explosive material as it was X-rayed.

There was something metal inside, that was the only indication of material. Nothing else. It was then scanned again and carefully opened.

"Sir," came a response from a military personnel.

"Sir, I need you to take a look at this," the master sergeant called to his superior officer, Captain James Beau Cannon.

The captain carefully removed the contents.

"If this is what I think it is, the U.S. Secretary of State along with the ambassador must be informed."

The package, as heavy as it was, was taken to the U.S. ambassador's office immediately.

"Sir," said the captain, "I'm not sure if this is just some of the plates or all the plates. The note says, 'Sorry for the inconvenience, the plates are all there, the currency has circulated back to the bank at no additional charge.'"

"These people have been playing with us for a long time. They have made a fool out of us. Get me the Australian PM on the phone. I want the Australian Federal Police to take these people and their operation down. I have the Secretary of State putting pressure on me to have this organisation brought to justice."

Hmm, brought to justice?

Alpha had carefully prepared the next step of winding down the tunnelling systems, collapsing some as they do in the coal fields underground, when finished in a certain area. Zulu had done a very powerful job in the planning and the construction, with all the support of the people Alpha had helped. Some of these people were mining engineers and fabricators.

The means of buying up houses from mortgage sales and giving them back to their rightful owners was one of Alpha's greatest ploys to get people on his side.

Some of the tunnels were built from the safe houses, uniquely designed so as they could never be picked up. Other tunnels that were decoy tunnels were built on a smaller scale to confuse the authorities in which direction and why they, the tunnels, were built that way.

Between Brisbane, Sydney and Perth, the excavations were complete. The safe houses were also in North Queensland where Lima's control hub was, and because the team was spread out across the country, it made it even more difficult for the authorities to detect them.

The law was the law but when those who are charged to uphold the law do not do their job and receive pay backs from those who manipulate it, it was time for the people to fight back.

This was Alpha's whole case.

The tunnels that were fabricated for getting people out and conveniently as well as storing containers of precious metals between double and false specially designed rock walls that would fit in with the surroundings was another great achievement.

But still the authorities did not know who Alpha, Lima, Foxtrot, Delta, and Zulu were. They only had Tango and this wouldn't be for very long, as Alpha had already designed an escape route in his careful planning. There was only a formal charge on her except the so-called association with a group of conspirators.

The mystery flyer was of great concern to Superintendent Jimmy Collins. No one saw him coming and no one saw him going, apparently. Not knowing he was to be taken off the case, as the U.S. State Department were insisting the Australian Federal Police were to take over. This was now an international crime. Not only had the banks been exposed for their corruption but also the federal reserves and the presiding governments.

The media had gotten a hold of some information that was extremely sensitive and they were able to expose more corruption and cover ups to do with off-shore government money laundering and bribe monies.

This would keep the authorities busy for some time, as they were dealing with Covid, Alpha and his team, and now exposed sensitive state and international dirty secrets.

Alpha had not known the Covid crisis would play into his plans.

The Federal Police in WA were becoming exhausted trying to interview as many fly-in fly-out workers as they could, but trying to get blood out of a stone, especially uncooperative people who were hidden behind face masks, just didn't seem like a good idea.

Alpha may or may not have been there.

But there was one fella who was keen to talk. This fella seemed to have no problems talking behind people's backs. Squealer or a snitch. He was after a reward at any cost and started talking. To those around him, they did not know where he got his information from but were concerned his actions would destroy the truth that the world was hearing.

Most of the nation had heard about Alpha and his operation. The community seemed to be on his side as he had exposed massive white-collar corruption, a job any state or federal government should have done. But a person with no known identity, just a code name Alpha, was righting the wrong, and if all his plans worked, he would expose the banks and governments and get away with it as well. This was a thorn in the state and federal police's side.

The snitch began talking. Talking about a man in a supervisory position, he didn't like this supervisor as he was always pointing out the truth to this man, "Bert." Bert had problems with alcohol and on several occasions he hadn't turned up for work. Bert also had an increasing drug problem and he believed a reward compensation would take him away from the people he despised.

This supervisor lived very quietly, Bert told the Police.

"You would only see him at work, never after, not even in the mess," so Bert claimed. "Most fellas you see either doing their washing, occasionally at dinner, even though you never sat with them. On fly out day, he was the last to get on plane and the first to leave, and then he was gone."

"Can we have a name?" the constable asked.

"He goes by the name of Ricky Martin."

The police constable interviewing Bert the snitch was taking every detail down. It would be the last they would see of Bert, as the company Bert worked for no longer required his services and he would not be employed in the industry again this far up the Pilbara.

He never received a reward for the information given to the police as it was only a name, no other details of this fella. So Bert not only lost out on a so-called reward (police would never pay out that amount), he also lost his integrity that day and self-respect.

The name was something the Western Australian and federal police could work on. They would now check the database nationally and fingerprint trace.

In the meantime, no one in the camp or onsite were willing to help the police with their enquiries.

The federal police were checking the mine site records of Ricky Martin. He didn't work directly for the mining company but as a contractor to a contracting company based out of Perth.

There was not much on the mining company's records except his up-to-date medicals, electrical licences and certificates, and the dates he had been onsite and that was it.

The contracting company in Perth were reluctant to give out personal information about any employee but were forced to by the Federal Police.

THE CHASE IS ON

Alpha had also prepared for this scenario and had Foxtrot delete all records on the contracting company's main server as a default.

Alpha would still be working for the contracting company at the refineries in South Perth when it just so happened the company server went down and his personal documents went down with it.

Having been caught between borders now for the last four months, Alpha was being as inconspicuous as possible in the public eye. Work at the refinery and back to the Air B'n'B at night, then changing format and in constant contact with the rest of the team through Foxtrot.

The old technology had paid off. It had completely confused the authorities, but the Federal Police were slowly piecing together the old radio transmission signals.

Alpha still had a bit of time with Delta in Perth to finalise the tunnelling system and passage of precious metals to the base of security.

Romeo was in his final stages of shipping the bullion under secrecy to Perth from Istanbul and he would have to find a flight out under Covid conditions.

Alpha had constantly been monitoring the conditions, especially when arriving through the WA border protection programme as this was changing on a week-to-week basis due to Covid.

The shipment was the final piece of the puzzle.

Customs and quarantine would be notified in WA of business purchases with this consignment of precious metals.

Foxtrot had the cameras and database programmes for WA customs and was making sure there would not appear any irregularities. Also, there was a customs senior officer working for the team and he was positioned to be there onsite when the shipment arrived.

The WA and Federal Police were going through all the mining charter flight manifests and dates to try and establish who this Ricky Martin was. Ricky was just a name to the contracting company, the HR would never have met him, they only had a voice to a name. A photo would have helped, but the servers for the company were down and it was expected some of the data could be lost.

How convenient, George Laban of the Australian Federal Police thought.

George had briefed all personnel that this was a national emergency and they were running out of time to catch Alpha and his team.

The unwillingness of the public to help was a thorn in the side, as this so-called Alpha had publicly exposed certain documents that should never have been released, concerning the financial institutions and reserve banks. How Alpha got this information was unknown to George, but he was about to find out when connecting directly to Alpha's improvised line.

"Alpha, George Laban, I've taken over from Superintendent Jimmy Collins from Queensland. You are now dealing with the Federal Police. Alpha, I want to make quite clear to you, that we are tracking you and your gang down and we will arrest you and the others."

"On what grounds, Commander? We laid our case quite openly to the Superintendent with no answer."

"International theft and money laundering, Alpha, and conspiring to break the country's financial institutions and reserve bank, not to forget wasting police time," said George Laban.

Keeping Alpha talking gave time to find the source of transmission. This was confusing to the Federal Police as transmissions were bouncing off different repeater stations right around the country. The Bushmen had done their job in some of the remote outbacks of Australia.

"Commander, who do you work for?"

"What sort of a question is that, Alpha?"

"Answer the question, Commander."

"We are a government body to protect the national interests of this country."

"So money laundering is a crime, Commander?"

"Keep him talking," said the Commander. "There must be some way we can trace this radio signal."

It was moving all the time, bouncing off repeater stations as well as very high transmitters.

"Commander, you had better arrest those CEOs in the banking institutions and reserve banks. In this Covid crisis, they have printed more currency than ever before and are expecting to get returns on it. I can imagine increased commodity prices and the poor consumer suffers. No currency is handed out without returns."

"You are a government body, swearing an oath to uphold the law, Commander. Do your job and we'll do ours truthfully. Good day, Commander."

"Anyone get anything on tracing that call?"

Alpha, now with Delta in Western Australia, was bringing his organisation closer together. He had the ears and eyes of Delta in state government and big businesses around the state. Delta would keep reminding Alpha the two most important rules: do things others won't do and it's not what you know, it's who you know.

Alpha had got the first stages of the plan completed.

1) Conveniently building the three main tunnels from three different cities in Australia from unidentified safe houses. (Decoy tunnels also to confuse authorities). These houses bought back and given back to those who had lost them from bank mortgage sales.

2) The training classes of all the personnel in transmission of radio calls and old cell phones that could be discarded.

3) The reprinting of $1 U.S. dollar to U.S. $100 dollar bills on authentic paper and authentic U.S. printing plates.

4) The currency to buy as much gold and silver as possible from gold merchants around Australia and Southeast Asia in big and small commodities.

5) He had a dress code for every person purchasing so that they didn't expose their face to the cameras.

6) The treasures placed in tunnels by operatives in areas uniquely disguised by false rock walls. The tunnels with escape hatches near convenient landmarks no one knew about.

7) Completely confusing the authorities on the team's identification.

8) An airline pilot who had been stood down from company due to Covid had become an operative and was using the outback' of Northwest Queensland to fly the transmitter below the commercial flight paths of schedule traffic.

9) Sending the U.S. $100 plates back to U.S. through their embassy in Sydney.

10) Always one step ahead of the authorities.

THE BIG ESCAPE

Centralising the operation with everyone involved and whilst the Federal Police were trying to track down identities, Alpha had set the big escape into motion.

This meant getting Tango out from police custody in Brisbane.

They really had nothing to charge her on.

At the same time, Alpha was trying to manage all his commitments at home back in Queensland. He had not allowed for Covid to cause this huge distance gap between his work activities and home.

You've heard of the story of the fella who went to the doctor with severe burns to his right ear. When the doctor asked how he got the burns, he replied, "I was ironing and watching television at the same time when the phone rang. I picked up the iron instead of the phone."

Puzzled, the doctor asked, "How did you get burns to your left ear?"

He exclaimed, "He called back."

When you've been burned by someone, be careful of being put in the same position of being burned over and over again.

Alpha had learnt from the above, that's why he planned so carefully over a period of time, allowing for every possible situation. His team, the authorities, the corruption, the heartaches families had to suffer, and now those who had taken advantage of the suffering through Covid.

All Alpha now wanted to do was go home to Mackay, Queensland,

❋

continue running his operation from there, and centralise and streamline every detail.

The federal police were trying to establish leads where this Ricky Martin lived and where he was working at present. There was an address in Perth that Ricky had maintained in Central Perth, but Delta the engineer would make sure all files or records in the hotel where Ricky Martin stayed would remain anonymous. No records would be found as Ricky Martin would always pay cash.

George Leban asked, "Who is this Ricky Martin?"

"There is no trace, no identity, all we have is a mine site security access card, with a partial photo." George was addressing his staff. "There are no fingerprints, a clean record, only a handful of people were in contact with him. One was involved in a mine vehicle crash, narrowly escaping with three others, at the end of the previous year during a cyclone."

George and the Federal Police were redirecting their enquiries now to the Perth area. They felt sure they would start to make some possible connections to establish new leads to who this Ricky Martin was.

George didn't know that Alpha (Ricky Martin) had Delta who was very influential with the authorities of WA. He was the eyes and ears for Alpha. Every decision being made through the authorities Delta had some knowledge about.

It was time to get Alpha back to Queensland.

THE MAN WHO NEVER WAS

Alpha had remembered a funny incident that happened at the Perth Airport a year or so ago when the company had booked flights to the Pilbara. The preferred airline to fly was Qantas Australia. However, for this particular flight, due to time tables, the company had booked Alpha on a Virgin flight from Perth to Port Hedland.

Having had very little sleep in the previous twenty-four hours, Alpha rocked up at the check-in counter and yes, the Qantas staff booked him on a flight and he wasn't to know it wasn't Port Hedland. There was a congratulations from Qantas staff on going platinum frequent flyer and a puzzled look on Alpha's face.

Tired, Alpha said, "I'm a gold frequent flyer member, how did I reach platinum status?"

Alpha was handed the ticket without looking at it and proceeded through security up to the Qantas lounge for a bit of refreshments and a shower, then to the departure gate.

Within an hour, and having spoken on the phone to his mother, the boarding call came. To Alpha's amazement, the boarding call at the gate number was not where he wanted to go.

Alpha looked at his ticket and the first name on the ticket was not his. Alpha's bags were on that plane and he had to get them off. In a rush, Alpha ran to the Qantas service desk. Seeing the ticket and the name on that ticket, the staff went into a massive panic.

This was a security breach an Alpha unwittingly had caught Qantas out. Alpha was thinking he would have liked to be on the receiving end with the fella who had issued the ticket.

Alpha (Ricky Martin) on the ticket (Russell Martin).

Alpha's company had to be notified. At first Joanne in the office could not stop laughing until the company had to have a new ticket re-issued at their expense and not the mining company's expense. That hurt a bit and the seriousness came out in Joanne.

It would be another three days before Alpha could reschedule his flight to be on a night shift at the port.

Meanwhile Jimmy (Delta), in those three days' downtime, had collected Alpha and had brought him to his office facilities to work on the operations and planning of the gold heist.

It was over a number of years this plan had been born and now the input from team members, such as Delta with his wealth of experience in the engineering and social status, was about to unfold.

Paul (Charlie) had kept a low profile in recent times. He was known as the SLEEPER and his preparation of organising transportation, ticketing, disguised names, and disposing of old equipment such as cars, motorcycles and push bikes.

Charlie now arranged all of Alpha's flight details. Charlie knew the Federal Police were looking for a Ricky Martin and were trying to track all his movements down, from flights, to hiring of vehicles, to where he accommodated himself in WA, to what other sites he had been working on. The Feds knew there was someone else working on his behalf, as files and locations had been deleted, persons involved in his industry were unwilling to help, and they were concealing evidence and persons could be charged if it was known that they were doing so. But still there was no real footage of this Ricky Martin, no national database that held his fingerprints, no one that really knew him. Or so it was thought.

The only person who had come forward was Bert the squealer, whose information was only a name, a trades person who was involved in a near washout on a mine's road months ago and could vaguely remember his features. These were the only items that the Federal Police could go on.

George Laban thought, *How could a professional person like this have kept himself so anonymous? He has no bank cards, no driver's license. He would have had to have some identification when applying for work. Alpha had to live, sleep, and eat somewhere. He's got to be going by another name. There must be a lot of national support behind this person. He couldn't rock up to any store purchase and say, "Hello, I'm Alpha and here's my ID. I would like to purchase this item." The proprietor would say, "Certainly, sir, let me go get the paperwork," and disappear out the back, only to inform the police or security that there was a strange man acting suspiciously on his premises.*

Alpha was far too smart for that. He would have studied people, camera layouts, accessible roads or streets. He would have planned every detail.

Alpha must be one of the cleverest persons George had ever come across. But clever people still have their weaknesses.

Then there was still Tango in police custody in Brisbane. A lawyer for her was insisting the state police release her, as no charges could be laid, on hearsay.

Alpha would be arranging to get her out and maybe make her disappear inside the organisation.

Charlie was arranging air tickets to get Alpha home. Alpha had now been over in Western Australia for over five months. He hadn't seen his wife, daughters and friends in that time except by carefully displayed video links set up by Foxtrot. Since he was finishing off maintenance projects in the refineries in South Perth and running every aspect of the heist with his capable team, Alpha was getting a little tired. The federal police were distributing online sketches of a person resembling Alpha. The main features were lacking, but there was a general outline.

Alpha and his team had really stepped on a few toes, from accessing U.S. $100 printed notes that exposed and infuriated the U.S. government and world bankers to buying tons of gold reserves. The authorities wondered how he managed to plan and do this with the people entrusted to him, and how and where did they manage to store it securely.

Alpha was also pushing for a proven medication HYDROXYCHLOROQUINE that was effective for and against Covid 19. Some of the medical profession said it wasn't a cure. Others said it was a strong medication, having been around for a while.

To push any vaccine that hadn't been clinically trialed was extremely reckless.

The world leaders knew a big reset in the currency world was coming, but they hadn't foreseen groups working on resistance and establishing true money and wealth to replace what the elite had stolen from the world over the years since the gold standard was broken.

The Nazis stole tons of gold from the Jewish people up through the 1940s, storing it and hiding it from the rest of the world. A big hall is still missing after seventy-five years.

These guys bought the gold with another country's currency and gave the printing press back to the rightful owners.

Alpha and the team were thought or estimated to have more bullion than most countries' wealth. The authorities worked these figures roughly from the consistent purchases of gold and tracking imports from around the world. A portion now from off shore markets was flowing through so called private enterprise but all seemed legitimate.

The authorities didn't know about Romeo being a part of the organisation in Turkey or any the consignments of precious metals he was to bring back. Romeo had to stay in Turkey for months to ensure every item was on that manifest on the ship, having to fly halfway around the world at his own expense at the time as the shipping company and authorities did not honour their agreements. A double portion had to be paid out to them.

However, Romeo maintained all the necessary medication and physio, medical expenses, and rents for him and his sister. This would be with the help of the Alpha team, who were glad to help.

One of the benefits of being part of the team was looking out for each other. As they would say in the mining industry where mental and physical issues can occur, "Look out for your mates." Typical Aussie slang. (Look out and look after your friends, as they would do the same for you.)

It wouldn't be long before Romeo was home to WA. This would be the final part of the puzzle.

Delta would run the operation and final completion of tunnels and exits, and storage of goods on the western side of this dry, great land.

Romeo could also deal with his sister's condition and help his only sibling to benefit from how he had become part of the Alpha team.

Charlie had managed to work on the Russell Martin identity for Alpha (the Qantas incorrect name on boarding pass, Russell Martin, came in handy) as the Federal and State Police were on the hunt for a fly-in fly-out worker Ricky Martin. A bogus reward of $250,000 that would never be substantiated out of the police budget was on the table, only to make people feel that it was real.

What the Federal and WA State Police didn't know was that the authorities were being infiltrated by Delta. His famous last words, "It's not what you know, it's who you know."

The timing and decisions made from the top was always surrounded by people like Delta who helped them make those decisions.

And so information was passed on interstate for Alpha and his colleagues.

An ID check at the airport Qantas check in would only be a positive ID from a driver's licence or passport and Russell Martin would be the name on the ticket, having been booked by Charlie.

Alpha spent five weeks at the nickel refinery, replacing hazardous and explosive switch gear and calibrating industrial instrumentation. The federal and state police had no further clues to his whereabouts. Then out of the blue, a person who had convinced himself he would get the police reward saw someone who roughly fitted that description in a supermarket in South Perth of the infamous Alpha.

This would happen to be the day Alpha was flying back to Queensland. Alpha had been shopping there but had not realised the person was watching him. Fortunately for Alpha, it was just a quick stop after work, and having packed his gear all up, he was heading to drop the rental car off at the Perth Airport.

Once again, the Federal Police lost the trail. The man being questioned by the police had not seen the car the person he had described got into. The only thing the police now had to go on could have been a rental car and they would have to go through all the rental companies to clarify a person of this description and name at the airport or in Perth City.

Alpha had picked this car up after hours and would deliver it back after hours to avoid any suspicion. The car had been rented out to a Jimmy Swagger and he was the second driver on the contract. Unless the contract was looked at very carefully, his name in small print was Russell Martin.

"A man should choose a friend that is better than himself. There are plenty of acquaintances in the world but very few friends."

Alpha drove the rental car back to the Perth airport and would leave on the red eye flight back to Brisbane. It was a very wise decision, Alpha being booked on the late flight as the next day state and federal police were swarming the Perth airport looking for any signs of this Ricky Martin. An APB had been sent interstate. The biggest problem was that it was mandatory for everyone to wear a face mask in the airport and on every flight. This would make a very slow process for the police to identify anyone resembling one Ricky Martin.

The public was following the Alpha team. It had become a national and international story and the public were coming to grips with the reality of the situation. Complacency and apathy is dangerous. Freedom comes with a price and must be fought for. If there was a one world government looming in the background, the people of each sovereign country had to band together and stand up for freedom in order to stop them.

The people of Australia had seen how a small team had banded together over the years and helped people in disadvantaged positions in recent times, taking on the authorities in an unorthodox way. Their actions could save an economy from being controlled by an elite group of organised people who, over a number of years, had conspired to become a world domination power.

Alpha left the Perth Airport at 11.30 p.m. that Thursday night, quietly and unassumingly. He had watched some of the news that night at the airport, the top story a man wanted for questioning in conspiring to defame the country's economy. Alpha thought, *Is that the best they could come up with?*

The public weren't having this, they were cheering Alpha and his team on.

No one could put a facial description to this mystery man. He was looming behind the scenes running an organised team, not organised crime.

As Alpha flew through the night, he monitored the Queensland borders, knowing they could be closed at any time due to the seriousness of Covid. Police, military, doctors and nurses were monitoring every person coming in from interstate. Paperwork had to be filled out, asking the same old questions:

Have you been a Covid area in the last twenty-four hours?

Have you been overseas in the last fourteen days?

Do you have any Covid symptoms?

Alpha knew the importance of keeping the face mask on for his disguise. He knew an APB had been put out on him interstate. Alpha had taken the liberty to shave his beard off at Perth Airport and remove his glasses as he would be travelling as Russell Martin.

Falling into a deep sleep on his way to Brisbane, Alpha was

dreaming of the security of his family and friends. He knew Lima would be there to pick him up, dressed discreetly and in an area where there were no cameras.

But what about his friend Tango? Alpha woke, a little startled.

Being in Perth over those five months, Alpha on many occasions would quietly go and sit in a cathedral and close his eyes and pray. The strength and solitude that came from trusting in a far greater power he acknowledged daily gave him the strength to see through each day.

Alpha reflected on the time his sister was seriously ill all those years ago. This day he had flown to work on the east coast of the North Island of New Zealand. There was a Māori chapel and he had quietly gone in and knelt down, praying for his sister and family in the quietness and solitude of the holy place. Quite often, God doesn't take the pain away but he equips you with the strength to go through that pain. Alpha's sister did heal over the years to recover from that sickness, but the scars would remain.

Alpha was drifting in and out of sleep over those five hours in the air. The Australian continent is big and until you have flown over, around it, or driven it, you would never know how big it was. Alpha wondered how much longer he would be travelling to work like this. There were a number of people in crisis depending on him, and Tango was one.

Lima had done a great job with security and surveillance, as had Foxtrot, with the flying and computer integration on various necessary government items, Zulu with the direction and structure of tunnels and closing down tunnels, Delta the eyes and ears of WA and providing for Alpha in accommodation, Tango who not only had been a fly on the wall but the master of disguises for all, Romeo who was instigator of off-shore funds, and lastly Charlie the man who provided and ascertained all viable transport and ticketing needed for all and disposing of any incriminating evidence.

There were also the outback bushman, who installed portable transmitters way high up; the farmers of North Queensland who provided the necessary aircraft for transmitters; and the people themselves under Alpha's care who had nearly lost all hope when hope was necessary.

Now he had the country of Australia behind him.

Nobody had identified him except those who knew him.

In Brisbane, in his outrage, Superintendent Jimmy Collins had purposely kept Tango locked up.

There were no incriminating charges and her lawyer was having to go to court to get a judge to authorise her release.

Jimmy Collins was planning to use Tango for bait to save face and maybe save his job. There were good cops trying to keep the oath they had sworn and there were bad cops like Jimmy who would go above the law. He himself had obstructed justice and tried to cover it up. His own men would have to take the fall with the beating and illegal detention of Tango to get information on the whereabouts of the rest of the Alpha team and Alpha himself. Jimmy had played this game of chess with Alpha and been backed into a corner. Most people, when they are backed into a corner, become defensive.

This was Superintendent Jimmy Collins. He became obsessed with taking Alpha down with any means possible and this would now mean outside the law.

Unfortunately for the Superintendent, he was going to be removed from his position.

The pressure had been too great from the state government, the federal government, and the U.S. State Department. For some people this can be a great challenge to deal with, but for people like Jimmy Collins, this ordeal was something he had never experienced in his policing career. It had become an obsession, to take down a gang who had outsmarted him in every way possible.

FAILING TO PLAN
IS PLANNING TO FAIL

The Qantas flight into Brisbane was in the final approach to land at Brisbane International. Alpha had woken as soon as the cabin crew had announced preparations for landing. Alpha had kept his face mask positioned so nobody could recognize him. He filled in all the Covid papers for entering Queensland online and would not have any holdups, supposedly.

The airbus A330 landed and taxied toward the airbridge. It wouldn't be long for the disembarking. Alpha had collected all his belongings and was prepared to move quietly through the concourse.

As they were walking up the ramp into and through the concourse corridor, Alpha couldn't believe what he saw. Military personnel and police in large numbers, checking everyone's papers. If they didn't have the forms filled out correctly, they were taken aside. Alpha's documents were in order. He was asked if he was a fly-in fly-out worker, where he had come from, what was he doing in Queensland and his occupation. The officer was checking his laptop, scrolling through photos. It was almost as if he was trying to put a profile together of Alpha.

"Please take off your mask," the officer said.

Alpha removed his mask. He had no beard or glasses and then asked the police officer what he was doing.

"We have reason to believe there is a fly-in fly-out worker from Western Australia who may have been on the flight you were on, who is on our most wanted list. You are listed as a tradesperson, sir.

Where have you been working?"

Alpha spoke with a pretend broad Scottish accent and said, "Young man, I have come from working at the nickel refinery in South Perth and have been waiting to get home to Queensland for the last five months. The Queensland government has just opened the borders for me to get home, and if you will excuse me, I have a relative waiting to pick me up."

The young officer gasped and stood back and with no hesitation let Alpha through, not even comprehending this was the very man the authorities were looking for.

Alpha placed his mask back on, moving quickly away from the checkpoint. His Scottish accent had come in handy.

Alpha went downstairs to pick his luggage and tool bag up from the carousel. Police were roaming the concourse downstairs as well. They were obviously looking for someone. When Alpha asked the person next to at the baggage carousel why the police were here, she replied, "Have you not heard the news over the last few weeks?"

"Alpha and his team have taken down the corrupt banking system and nobody knows what he actually looks like or where he is," another person nearby added. "Rumour has it he was on a flight from the west and police are trying to identify a Ricky Martin who they believe to be Alpha."

"The public is behind him," said another.

"We will support him and the team," said another.

Then some loud cheering: "Ricky! Ricky! Rick!" Right on the ground floor of the terminal came the chanting. The police dogs were barking as the police tried to quieten the noise, which seemed to get louder and louder.

Alpha couldn't wait to get out of the terminal. He moved quickly to and through the front automatic doors and bent over, gasping for breath. Someone came to his aid and asked if he was ok.

Alpha collected himself, thanked the lady for her concern and said he had been on a long flight. He was very tired and anxious and glad to be going home after being caught between borders for five months.

The lady helped Alpha up, smiled and wished him a great day. Alpha replied in the same manner. He was so overwhelmed with the goodness he saw in people around him, he made a promise to himself he would always fight for that freedom, no matter the cost.

KEEP CALM AND FIGHT FOR FREEDOM

THE HOMECOMING

Lima was waiting at the other end of the undercover car parks at Brisbane domestic airport, where he said he would be with no obvious cameras.

"Lima, my good friend." Alpha shook his hand and gave him a big hug.

Lima helped Alpha with his bags, placing them in the boot of the car. There were police checkpoints at the perimeter of the airport, but it would not be obvious to any police at those checkpoints that the man they were looking for would be in this car with Lima. Alpha had his mask on. It was only the driver's ID they were checking.

Then they were away on the ten-and-a-half-hour road trip to Mackay. The trip by car was to reduce any amount of suspicion. The authorities were trying to close in on Alpha and his team.

The truth is, they were still clutching at straws.

The police in Queensland had been door-to-door searching for the safe houses in Mackay and Brisbane.

The police had tried to apprehend a rogue pilot or pilots who were using their aircraft as transmitters in Northwest Queensland and Northern Territory, flying below the flight paths of commercial traffic and out of Brisbane and Melbourne radar. The police themselves flew their own government plane to two cattle stations where they thought these fellas were operating from. But they were outwitted, wasting more of the state police budget.

The police tried to identify the type of transmitters for communication but were unsuccessful as the technology was World War

Two technology. There were not many people around who knew how to use this equipment anymore except specialised people such as Alpha and his team.

Then there was the hunt in WA for a Ricky Martin, a fly-in fly-out worker to the Pilbara who had simply vanished. Company records had been conveniently lost.

The national data bank showed no known ID but a number of Richard Martins spread all over the country except Queensland.

There were no fingerprints, no matching DNA, as there was nothing to take a sample of DNA from.

Then there was the mysterious return of the U.S. $100 plates to the U.S. Embassy that really aggravated the U.S. State Department, who wanted a full enquiry how those plates were obtained.

The exposure of the bank corruption in Australia and around the world had caused the Australian government to make official enquiries into the banks' recklessness in recent years.

People were becoming more attuned to real money, gold and silver bullion that had been traded for over five thousand years with no problems. This was God's resources not man's corruption.

Why did it have to take a group of people who were very much concerned about complacency and apathy setting in around the world that allowed the few to control the majority?

Alpha just wanted to remain anonymous, he didn't want the applause or the accolades. He wanted ordinary people to live the life they could freely choose, with liberty, great courage, and everybody on an even playing ground. That, and he wanted to go home.

His wife, family and friends would be waiting for him. It wasn't a time to be complacent as the one quick slip could put him in checkmate.

The ten-hour drive home to Mackay would give Alpha the chance to recollect his thoughts and communicate with Lima the next part of the plan.

Lima had maximised security with Foxtrot's help. The three safe houses in Mackay and two in Brisbane had been designed with cameras in the most obscure places, as they could not be seen, but they could pick up every movement of animal, human or car within thirty-five meters at every angle.

The tunnels Zulu had maintained in North Queensland and Brisbane as well as the smaller tunnels in Sydney and WA were finished. The wall linings for storing the safe passage of bullion and emergency food provisions and accommodation were all built carefully to design. Areas of the tunnels that were not required, especially from decoy safe houses and decoy tunnels, were collapsed. This would confuse authorities even more.

The more time getting ahead of the authorities in every possible way, the more their budgets would blow out.

Every person under Alpha's leadership had a skill that was so important to the plan. And everyone began to have new hope. This wasn't just a plan, this was a plan that had taken a number of years to prepare. The preparation of every foreseeable problem, actions made by the authorities, the actions of anything that would upset the team or persons under Alpha and his care.

Now they had a plan for Tango, and to get her out.

Alpha and Lima had passed all the checkpoints out of Brisbane. There were digital boards with a rough description of Ricky Martin, with the authorities in desperation saying they were looking for this man, and to please contact your nearest police station if you had any information.

The crowds that gathered to hear the updated news on the Alpha team were applauding. This quiet reserved person no one had seen in public was fighting for them and although the circumstances with the Covid crisis was causing havoc with lockdowns and world finances, here in Australia alone, people began to have hope that the truth would come out.

The Americans were angry, and the Australian and state and federal governments were in a state of flux.

The countries' reserve banks had printed more currency than ever before to try and bail themselves out and keep their economies going. Businesses here in Australia had seen tough times before, but with total lockdowns here in this great country and around the world, businesses were laying off staff, not knowing if anything would become normal again.

Foxtrot had felt this grief flying the Qantas routes on the A330 Airbus into some Asian countries three months prior. And speaking with Alpha that day arriving in NZ prior for Christmas, Foxtrot had expressed his views.

"The past cannot be changed, edited, or erased. It can only be accepted. What you learn from it gives you the power to move on and better."

Through those ten hours of driving through to Mackay, the plan to rescue Tango was readied for action. Alpha had planned for every situation without the opposition having a clue what the plan was. The knights and the bishops were moving forward on the chess board.

The public was on the Alpha team's side. All they knew is things had gone from bad to worse, but things could not get any worse

This was a reprieve for them, it was like a story or an epic movie they were following and they themselves were involved in it.

In the central police station in Brisbane, operations had placed their full attention on hunting down Ricky Martin. They were not paying much attention to Tango who they had locked up in custody.

Alpha had the premonition of what would happen. He had explained this to everyone in the preliminaries before the operation.

Ryan, the plain clothes police officer with Jack, had also aired his opinions on the matter with Tango to the Superintendent Jimmy Collins, but it had fallen on deaf ears.

Ryan would be the officer who would quietly take Tango out of the holding cell with the excuse she would be going in for more questioning, but in the process would release her way outside the Police Headquarters. There was an area the camera footage outside the station had a slightly limited coverage. Ryan had proved that on several occasions when taking persons into custody. He had queried this, but nothing had been done about it.

Just like Peter in Biblical days, the passionate prayer of friends prayed for his release from prison.

An angelic being sent, came, released his chains, opened the jail doors while everyone was asleep, and led Peter out.

When he arrived at the house of those who had been praying for his release, they were so overjoyed, they forgot to let him in.

This was the perfect opportunity for him to release her. All he could say was that he had taken her for more questioning in the interview room, which he did, and returned her to her cell, which he did. Tango was quietly moved, told nothing, but was taken to the rear of the building, escorted by Ryan who never said a word. He then proceeded to take her down the back of a side street, Tango asking him where was taking her. Turning the next corner, Ryan, seeing Tango's battered face and arms, said, "You're on your own, sweetheart," turned, and went back the way he came.

Very surprised and puzzled, Tango knew she couldn't use her phone but proceeded to the nearest safe house fifteen or so kilometres away. She had to walk in and out of back streets, but she did it.

Tango knew where all three safe houses were.

Alpha's plan had worked.

An hour or so later, the duty officer went to check on Tango's cell. Peering through the door hatch, he saw no Tango. The Brisbane Central Station went into full lockdown. A prisoner had escaped without a trace. There was no damage in the cell, the camera footage showed her leaving the cell and returning to the cell with the young detective Ryan Shad-Bolt, and then nothing unusual after that.

The outside cameras were checked at all locations around the station but nothing unusual once again.

What the technicians did find was that a certain camera had not given full coverage on one corner of the building near an exit door, and looking at their job lists previously, there was a job to replace that camera as Detective Ryan Shad-Bolt had complained that bringing persons into custody, there had been no full coverage at that point.

There were questions around that time Detective Ryan spent with Tango and he would be scrutinised, as he was the last to see her.

Superintendent Jimmy Collins had been stood down, as his inappropriate behaviour had got the better of him. The new Superintendent replacing him, John Holland, was a little more cool-headed and not sadistic under pressure as Jimmy Collins.

He interviewed Detective Ryan at great lengths. What was he doing interviewing this Tango, what questions was he asking, and what was he trying to find out?

Detective Ryan Shad-Bolt was a good police officer and had an extremely good record.

"Ryan, what were you trying to prove? Did you get some more Information out of her with less beatings from Jimmy Collins?"

"How the Superintendent Jimmy Collins had dealt with Tango towards the end was appalling. All I did was assure her that what happened under Jimmy Collins was going to be followed up on. I asked if she was going to make a formal complaint on her treatment and amazingly she said no. Bruised and battered a little, I left her and that was the last I saw of her. The cameras can confirm that." The camers did confirm that. But they did not show everything.

Ryan was a very quiet reserved man and although an officer of the law had known when an injustice was done.

Detective Ryan Shad-Bolt knew that the Superintendent Jimmy Collins had a personal vendetta against Alpha, as Alpha had out-smarted him in every way possible and it seemed like the new Superintendent John Holland would not make anything better, except he wouldn't take the law or hold a personal vendetta in his own hands.

The Covid crisis had stabilised, but people were still living in that fear of what if. What if we lose our jobs, our security, our homes, or Covid hits us again?

Alpha had arrived back in Mackay with some of the team quietly applauding him.

Tango had cleverly disguised herself after reaching the number one safe house and would quietly disappear into the realms of the Alpha team, but she remained a little puzzled why she was released secretly by Detective Ryan Shad-Bolt.

The dream of freedom had only begun and it was catching on around the country of Australia and hitting the global scene.

Economies were being destroyed by an instigated virus, but people had seen what a group of people could do in this present environment and were fighting back.

Alpha and his team, the few around the country and the world, knew what was coming and it wasn't going to be pretty.

Preparation over these last ten years had been the key with wisdom from above.

RIGHTEOUSNESS EXALTS A NATION

—PROVERBS 13:14

Where Alpha got the U.S. money plates was still a mystery and he hadn't revealed it. But the irony of it all was that the few who manipulated the world economic systems and had been stealing from the world economies for years intentionally would now get their own back from those they had manipulated from. People of most nations were crying out for a sense of accountability, justice, values and God-given liberty for every man, woman and child.

Storing up treasure was not an issue, being accountable and sharing the concerns of people in all walks of life was the issue.

"Rivers do not drink their own water; trees do not eat their own fruit; the sun does not shine on itself; and the flowers do not spread their fragrance for themselves. Living for others is a rule of nature. We are all born to help each other. No matter how difficult it is, life is good when you are happy, but much better when others are happy."

Alpha was just happy to be home with his wife, who he still frustrated at times with his outlandish ideas, but always knowing they would work and seeing his grown young ladies that he hadn't seen for all those months.

Home now, his wife called him Ricky and only his close friends and neighbours who kept his identity safe, as they too (Alpha) had been working for them. It's what Ricky did with his team that made the difference.

Ricky never thought what he could not do but only what he could do to help set people free.

✸

Ryan the detective had secretly made contact with him, advancing his concerns on this whole crisis, with the authorities blowing everything out of proportion. Ryan knew what the police were doing was unethical and he didn't want to go down that track. He still had a job to uphold the law, a family to protect, but he knew that Alpha had broken a law when it came to foreign assets. Without compromising his own moral code, Ryan also knew what was involved to save the integrity of the people and his own country, which he loved, and the price for freedom.

A thought came to Ryan from Dietrich Bonhoeffer, a book he had read about a famous German theologist martyr from the Second World War. "Which is worse, to do evil or be evil?"

Dietrich, a highly respected minister, twice shut down by the Gestapo, had been involved in the plot to assassinate Adolph Hitler at the closing months of the war. He was eventually arrested, tried and hanged in a prison within days of Germany's surrender.

Dietrich's conscience had bothered him as he was saving Jewish lives over the period the Nazi regime was in control of the German government as well.

Detective Ryan wasn't living under a nationalist socialist government, but there seemed to be a sense of manipulation from overseas control and slowly government control in Australia that concerned him. Ryan had spent nearly sixteen years in the Queensland police, and had lived in remote areas with his wife and children in rural Queensland. Ryan had seen some of the hardest criminals and gang confrontations that he and his colleagues had had to deal with.

Ryan had dealt with bush fires, emergency evacuations and flooding in recent times, but nothing had prepared him for these months with the Covid crisis and Alpha with his Gold Heist.

The police operations were a mess both in the state and federal scene. They had also been challenged by the U.S. Government regarding stolen property, although it had been returned.

The laws of prosecution in Australia were based on the English judicial system and its sovereign rights protected Australia under international law. But the Australian government still had extradition rights between the U.S. and Australia, if it so wished to go down that track, but if it did, the country would be up in arms. Alpha and his team would eventually make history in the events that were to come.

As for Detective Ryan, he was of two minds, whether to resign or stay and face the harsh reality of facing further questioning and scrutiny from John Holland and his colleagues.

Ryan thought, *Become so confident in who you are that no one's opinion, rejection, or behaviour can rock you.*

Ryan decided to stay on. His integrity would remain intact even when his colleagues would turn a blind eye to something that was not right. He also made up his mind he was not going to pursue Alpha and the team as he would need them later. Ryan knew what was coming and his family would also need Alpha's support.

Detective Ryan Shad-Bolt arrived at Brisbane Central to be bombarded with a load of questions in regards to the Tango escape.

"Ryan?" John Holland asked. "We had a direct link to the Alpha team through this Tango or whatever her name is and she has disappeared mysteriously. You were the last person to see her and we still need some answers. In between the hour that had passed from you, sir, and the duty officer checking in on her, someone let her escape."

"Jack, your partner was not there to confirm your story, only the cameras to and from the cell tell your story, Ryan. I think you let her escape."

"Service records show you complained about a faulty camera when bringing in a previous detainee that was covering an area of the yard, and hadn't been fixed in recent days. This gave you the opportunity to release her. Why?"

Ryan stood there for a moment and looked around. There were about five senior officers looking at him. He then said, "Are you accusing me with only circumstantial evidence?"

Then John Holland said, "Ryan, you were the very last person to see Tango, we are accusing you on suspicion. I need you to stand down on full paid until a full investigation has been made. I will need your badge and side arm."

Have the courage to follow your heart and intuition. They somehow know what you truly want to become.

STAGE FOUR OF THE PLAN
PUT INTO ACTION

Alpha was at home now with family, his neighbours and friends. Alpha was also in contact with the whole team. Foxtrot was in Mackay with Zulu and Lima, Tango was on private transport under-cover to Mackay. Charlie remained in Sydney anonymously. Delta was holding the fort in Perth and Romeo was on his way back from Turkey with the shipment of bullion to Western Australia. Romeo had been away from home for nearly a year, as in the first quarter of the year with Covid looming, his sister had been involved in a terrible accident in Sydney. Rachel had suffered terrible injuries and he had had to help deal with the hospitalisation process.

The team and people who had relied on Alpha were together. Everyone was safe and Alpha wanted to keep it that way.

The ransom was still on Alpha and his team's heads, but the problem now for the authorities was that their budget was running low. They had tried to track the Alpha team down all over Australia, and to a point there were groups now being established in other parts of the world who were now dismantling the plans of the one world order and a one world government. The people of the world were beginning to believe once again in the sovereignty of their own nations and developing nations and they wanted to take back their lands, their ideals, and their values from the corruption and manipulation of the few. This wasn't a state of socialist or commu-nist dictatorships, people were wanting the freedom and liberties that had been enjoyed in the past, that their forefathers had fought for and were now trying to be dismantled.

The problem looming was a big reset coming: the so-called monetary system was about to collapse due to corruption, there was no doubt about that. Alpha had come clean on that with establishing his team and groups of people to survive this very nasty blow. He would also fight for others if they were not so complacent.

In the operation centre in Brisbane and Sydney, the police were now placing a high priority on narrowing down locations for Alpha and his team. There was another problem. Alpha's organisation was spread out so far across Australia and had growing momentum. He could be anywhere and he was not driven by force or arms trade, Alpha was only driven by a simple idea which the authorities could not understand. This was the restoration of this great country's economy, the caring and the rights of all people, and prosperity for all persons if they choose under good leadership, one nation under God.

Alpha knew you had to fight a lot of battles before you win the war.

Superintendent John Collins was having none of this. This Alpha person had broken the law and it had an effect on one of senior staff Detective Ryan Shad-Bolt, so he thought.

John Holland and George Laban from the federal police were running out of options. They were having to give an account to the political constituents, state and federal governments, with no concrete results. Time was running out for the state and federal police to shut down the Alpha team. Gold merchants were completely out of stocks of bullion and would take some time to replenish stocks from the national mints of Australia. They were also being carefully watched by the authorities as no more would be sold only as government stock, and that wasn't much.

The army had been called in to help the police on a national scale, not only with the Covid crisis now but to catch and apprehend Alpha and his team at airports, wharfs, state borders.

Yet no one knew what he looked like, he could be disguised as anyone. He had removed any form of DNA and his work profile had been conveniently deleted. Even the rest of his team, apart from Tango, were unidentified.

There was no willing person apart from those snitches with limited information willing to come forward. It was like Alpha was under protective custody by the nation.

From the cities to rural areas of Australia, communities were stepping up their defiance in support of the Alpha team, which had exposed so much secrecy on a national and international level, the people that had voted governments in were shocked at what they were learning.

People around Australia were learning that their way of life could be taken away from them, with the collapsing of private enterprises, businesses and the free markets through Covid.

A broadcast had come out live on a few central city digital screens though Brisbane, Sydney, Melbourne, Perth with this message.

"We are called to serve not to be served, Alpha."

There was massive cheering and applauding.

Alpha would take no credit for this, he saw it as a means of serving through God's generous grace to him. He was no one special, just in the right place at the right time and in the right circumstances. Obviously, these circumstances and times in human history were becoming very dangerous for humanity worldwide. Alpha and the team had now a small window of opportunity to finish what they had started.

The tunnels and storage of bullion, food and supplies were complete and effectively hidden. The people and those they would screen were building, to become part of the organisation. Alpha still had a plan for those who were in desperate situations financially who were not with his organisation. Years of planning for every dark situation was coming to fruition and mental toughness would be required.

Success is universal for how much time Alpha and the team had invested over the years.

No one had stolen his dream. He had believed it would work

through those seven years of planning.

He was willing to take whatever it took. No one was going to steal the dream he had fought so hard for. He would have the courage to fight on for as many people as he could.

Never forget three types of people in your life:

1) Those who helped you in difficult times.
2) Those who left you in difficult times.
3) Those who put you in difficult times.

Romeo had all the consignments of bullion heading for a port north of Perth. A pick up at the port had been arranged by one of Alpha's loyal contracting businesses that would transport the consignment to a location inland and then Delta would move the consignment to its final destination with another preferred carrier.

Delta unknowingly had someone in the WA state government pick up on some unusual activities in a couple of meetings he had attended. There were some very sensitive questions about some business activities that he would not answer.

Politicians are usually suspicious of political opponents and in many cases use any thread of juicy information to discredit some person they find distasteful or don't agree with. Delta happened to be on the chopping block without him knowing it. But he would have a back stop. Delta also would have a plan B for any emergency situation. Being a successful businessman over the years and having made good ethical decisions, he would never have to look over his shoulder to have anyone catch him out with corruption or false pretence.

A certain politician had advised the Western Australian Police force seniority to prioritise their activities and monitor Jimmy Sapen (Delta).

Jimmy had taken the initiative and doubled the same transport company with two different wharf pickups. He himself would be overseeing the Perth pick up of cargo inventory from the wharf containers once they went through customs.

The shipment coming to Carnarvorn port was the shipment of

bullion no one knew about and port authorities were inspecting containers of furniture and metal infrastructure coming in from Turkey via the UK.

Foxtrot had made sure their hand scanners would not pick up metals other than steel and steel fibre. It was a clever move on his behalf. Technology can either work for you or work against you. It was just a matter of switching codes online.

The transport company had been briefed on specific remote roads to access and move the consignment as quick as possible onto another form of transport. This was all under cover of darkness.

These are the people who had gained Alpha's trust. He had supported some of these essential services in their darkest hours of Covid, maintaining operations with backup finance to keep their staff employed. This was done through Delta's force on the west coast.

Delta's men had arrived at Fremantle Port. The ship had berthed early that morning, a fresh August morning. Customs had been through the consignments with dog sniffers looking for illegal substances, things smugglers would deliberately hide in linings of anything that would stand up in a box shape.

It was now 16.40 p.m. on a Thursday afternoon. The port had been notified of an urgent consignment that had to be picked up no later than 17.30 p.m. that night. A special handling fee had been made as usually freight could not be collected for at least two to three days after having arrived in port.

All sorts of clearances and checks had to be approved.

The supervisor of the wharf store was advised well in advance that Jimmy Sapen (Delta) was coming in to collect his consignment through a transport company.

Delta's transport company had just got clearance access through security gate at the port with a heavy vehicle and trailer.

Watching from a distance was the commander of the Australian Federal Police, George Laban. He had a team of armed offenders with him to secure the premises and search the vehicle that had just entered the port facilities.

As the automatic gates at the
entrance were about to close, the
sirens of the police vehicles started
screaming. Two unmarked police
cars and a heavy armed offender's
van came screaming through the
gates, as they remained open for the
police vehicles.

Down at container twenty, the
truck had dropped its tailgate, also
on the trailer. As the fellas were

about to load the consignment, the police cars and van came
roaring down the road access towards the truck then came to an
abrupt halt.

George Laban got out of the police car.

"Stop all loading, those containers are under investigation, this
area is now under police custody."

The detectives and armed offenders had unlocked all two containers. With lights and torches, they were pulling everything out
of the containers and stripping down boxes, furniture, and steel
components bit by bit.

The driver and one his colleagues were asking the questions.

"What are you looking for specifically, Inspector?"

A muffled voice came back saying, "We believe these containers
are carrying some specific items, aiding a criminal organisation."

Looking at the consignment paper work, the inspector got a
shock of his life. These containers had come through from New
Zealand and the items were for Bunnings warehouse.

This cannot be, George said to himself. *We've been misled. There
must be another port on the western seaboard with containers having come through from Turkey or western Europe.*

"I want the manifest of every shipping consignment that has
reached Australian ports from Europe in the last forty-eight hours,"

George Laban yelled. "Pack it in here, everyone, we're going."

Very disgruntled, George Laban and his band of merry men left the port, leaving the carrier company to repackage and load stock onto trucks.

The driver then rang and advised Delta of what had just happened.

Always have a plan B. Delta knew someone in the chain of command had been disgruntled with him and was out for blood.

Meanwhile the freight company had left Geraldton Port and was off road now to the rendezvous drop off point eighty kilometres inland from Geraldton.

Ten minutes away, they would see some bright lights in the distance, the pickup point for the consignment. There was a mechanical lift on the side of the truck to unload and transport the pellets onto the next truck. This could be managed quite quickly with a quick departure to follow. The second truck was on its way to the deposit location, a designated area that Delta and Zulu had assigned (the entrance camouflaged to the tunnel in Perth.)

Romeo was on the long flight back from Turkey via Debi and Singapore back to Perth. He had seen the shipment off and made sure all the paper work for the consignment was in order and nothing left unaddressed this time. He would meet up with Delta and Zulu in Perth.

Zulu had flown from Queensland to New South Wales to Western Australia to check and make sure that all the tunnels and equipment were sound and secure. All the provisions were there and the entrances and exits were unidentifiable to anybody except those who had built them.

This was a remarkable achievement for the whole team, friends and their families.

Romeo knew he would have to endure the fourteen days of quarantine in Perth at a designated hotel. Delta would keep in contact with him until the fourteen days was finished and then take him to

join the rest of the team. Perth was Delta's base and he would ensure all communications with the team and the tunnel base would
be kept a top priority.

Delta knew the federal and state and a matter of fact all states of
Australia police enforcement were trying to piece the trail together
of the Alpha team. It was a desperate race of time and resources
to piece the whole puzzle together and time was not on their side.

Tempers were flaring in every police operations centre in the
country. The few that came forward with scattered information
about the Alpha team were seen as informers who were after a slice
of the reward that was dangling like a carrot in front of them.

George Laban had all the information of ships that had berthed
at ports in WA and found the ship he had been looking for. The ship
called the Arvin had berthed at the port of Geraldton three days
before, arriving from Istanbul, Turkey. The police had contacted the
port customs and authorities to stop all shipments of goods leaving
the port as a federal investigation was going to take place as of
now, police closing all access until investigation was complete.

What George Laban hadn't been advised earlier, the transport
company had taken out the consignment the night before.

As the police had locked every container down at the port pend-
ing investigation, George Laban and the chief inspector from the
WA police force Cyril Bradwell were flown into Geraldton on the
eastern seaboard north of Perth.

"What information have you got on the containers?" George
Laban asked Cyril from the WA police.

"George, we got another slight problem, the contents of the
containers we are looking for were shipped out last night by a
transport company and we don't know where."

"Damn," George shouted.

"Get me that transport company online now. I want the manifest
and where it went. I want the drivers and the company dispatch
manager detained for helping with enquiries, is that clear?"

The race was on. The unmarked police vehicle hit the curb as they pulled into the transport company yard in Stockland Street, Geraldton.

The big sign overlooking the street said, "Wards, Carriers, and Transport Services." A number of heavy vehicles were loading and unloading consignments when the police moved in.

George and Cyril marched straight into the office, not offering good mornings, instead snapping, "Police, this office and manager with drivers asked for are under investigation. I want the manifest for the last forty-eight hours and the drivers of those trucks here in this office now."

"Officer, some of those drivers are on the road now and hundreds of kilometres away," said Bruce Blomfield, the area manager.

"I want them stopped, pulled up. We'll get the police in the area to detain them. I don't care how it's done, stop them."

The manager and the drivers in the office were being harshly interviewed.

"I want to look at the manifests of the three trucks going south last night," George Laban screamed at the manager.

"And you lot, where did you stop on the way? I want a statement from every one of you before you leave this office."

"The manifest shows stocks going to warehouses in small locations south of Geraldton, one place being Exeter. I see other stops down to Perth."

"All the stop offs are Bunnings, Miter 10, the tool shed, the warehouse, but where is my shipment of bullion, Bruce? Who drove that shipment off road and where?"

Outside the gates of the transport company, a number of people were gathering, then a larger group spread down the street. Word had got around the community that their trucking company was being interrogated by the police. The premises were being circled by the community.

Then the chanting started: "Federal Police, get out of our community and leave us in peace."

The more people came, the more the situation became tense.

"George, you got take a look at this. You may have to call for back up," said Cyril Bradwell.

George raced to the window, flustered from not getting the results he wanted. He shouted, "We are not finished here, if we have to take your drivers into custody we will now, so call the mob off, Bruce."

The country of Australia was in a state of change. It was like a peaceful revolution.

No one wanted violence. People just wanted their voices to be heard.

The people wanted their liberty and free markets, not markets controlled by the few.

The Alpha team had stood for the people and they were being hounded by an unfair justice system.

The police, who had swarmed in to uphold the law and protect the people, had created an adverse effect.

George Laban and Cyrillic Bradwell weren't all about the law. They were out for revenge as they, like Jimmy Collins, had been outsmarted by a few ordinary people.

"This is official federal police business. Any one interfering or obstructing justice will be arrested."

A voice called out, "Then you will have to arrest all of us here, as we are not moving until you yourselves decide to leave."

Fuming now, as there were only two unmarked vehicles and one armed offender's van and no back up as yet, George would not fall victim to the crowd. His pride was about to be shattered as the crowd moved in.

A voice cried out, "If you use force on unarmed and peaceful civilians, you will be filmed not only on national news but international news as well. See the cameras now and phones videoing the scene."

George was now forced into a corner. They would have to leave. This was a very unusual scene for the federal police. Usually a riot brought violence, but this was a peaceful protest for the backing of a local transport company and its drivers.

George made the decision to leave the transport office with the documentation. In his mind, this would not be the end. He would return with force and would shut the company down.

The police vehicles moved through the crowd. There was no booing, just a look of satisfaction and smiles on the faces of the people who supported their community and businesses.

George Laban was struggling to figure out why the backup was late in arriving.

Nothing like this had ever happened before. People were unified in all walks of life. It wasn't threatening or damaging to anyone, these were marches of concern.

And the bullying tactics of the federal and state police didn't help.

Delta had seen what was happening up at Geraldton from satellite news link, and as soon as the feds and state police had left, he radioed Bruce Blomfield through the special VHF transmitter set that the police could not intercept.

Bruce was ok, a little shaken but thankful Delta had made contact. Bruce was also overwhelmed by the community support. These were ordinary everyday people who made a stand on the values and the business they cared about. This trucking business had given back to the community many times over the years and now it was the community that would stand with Wards, Carrier and Transport Services.

The drivers interviewed were also a little shaken by the bullying tactics by the police force.

Two drivers had been briefed the night previous by management about their drop off on a dirt road. If questioned they would stick to the covered consignment details to the drop off points of Bunnings, Miter 10 and other local businesses for communities south of Geraldton, picking up freight for the mining companies on their return trip.

Covid rules and regulations on this side of the Australian continent were forever being increased as outbreaks or so-called out breaks of Covid gave the premier an excuse to close the WA border.

But to Delta, "He who laughs last has the last laugh."

Delta's main concern now after the ordeal up north was to get Romeo to a Covid hotel for his fourteen days of quarantine. He then would be shifting him to a safe house, then relocating him to Queensland for a time to debrief with Alpha.

Romeo's plane would arrive from Singapore in the early hours of a May morning.

Being away for over a year and coming back to Australia to be a caregiver for his sister was going to be a big ask for Romeo.

His assignment for collectively buying the gold and packaging it up consistently in Turkey had been one of the remarkable things the Alpha team had put together.

Shipping documentation, having to pay twice for the incompetence of sending consignments and the wrong consignments, incurring a trip to New Zealand and accommodation expenses under Covid requirements—Romeo's rewards were coming. Living all that time out of a hotel room, and negotiating purchasing deals with the sellers and at times with a no compromising attitude, had made him very weary. The thought of sleeping in his own bed, eating his own favourite home-cooked foods, and seeing friends he had been isolated from due to Covid and lockdowns in Istanbul for so long was comforting.

Romeo had been robbed at gunpoint at a money machine in Istanbul. He had to hand over some thousands of dollars as he was about to purchase goods.

People here were under lockdown, with no incomes and watching the streets very carefully to rob those who had money. Romeo thought, *Has the world really come to this?*

The will to succeed in life is important, but what's more important is the will to prepare.

Detective Ryan Shad-Bolt was disillusioned with the state and federal police force. He was now suspended with a formal investigation on his activities of the last week in Tango's escape.

His wife and children knew Ryan as a good man and gave him all the support he needed.

Ryan knew he couldn't go back to the force. He would be scrutinised and given a desk job forever.

What John Holland was planning to do was unethical. The state government had required him to use any force measurable to bring in Alpha and his team.

One thing the force had forgotten was they had been backed into a corner on the chessboard. It was nearly a checkmate with Alpha on final play.

Alpha had not only the people of Queensland on his side but the nation. He also had the interests of many other nations watching.

Alpha was playing the game out a little longer and not wanting to bring the police force down, he just wanted to weed out the corruption that was consuming them by the few who were dominating the majority and this came from the higher levels of government.

There was only one final decision Ryan could make. He would sacrifice in the short term but in the long term he, his family and others would benefit. Ryan had to join the Alpha team. No questions about it.

Ryan loved his country, its values and its people, and he was seeing a state-run system coming with freedoms removed. A police state.

Ryan had sworn as a police officer to hold up the values, to protect the public, to ensure the rights of all people were adhered to and to uphold justice for all.

This simple thought came to Ryan, *Your decisions shape your destiny.*

A wrong decision can have significant consequences.

Tango had left a contact address number on a piece of paper and had slipped it into Ryan's hand just before they parted. He still had it with him in his coat pocket. Now was the time to utilise that contact for him and his family.

Ryan knew the street was about five kilometres away from the central Brisbane CBD. He also knew that Tango never once in her interrogation had allowed herself to fall to the level of those who were questioning her. She had kept her cool even when yelled at and verbally abused.

Tango would rather have thought of something funny, which infuriated John Holland and Jack Race, Jack being or had now been his partner till handing in his badge and side arm.

Smile and forgive. It's the only way to live. This was Tango.

This had kept a smile on her face as she parted ways with Ryan a week before.

Ryan knew he could trust Tango if he could make contact with her and so he went looking for the house.

He did not realise at first that he was being tracked by his phone's GPS system and the police had also been watching his home and movements to and from. He finally started to think about his position. He was stood down but the thought came to him about being watched. Ryan would have done the same thing if positions were reversed.

Ryan ran every back street he could find. He had been training for a long distance run in recent months and this could be one of his long-distance runs. He threw his phone aside and jumped every fence he could. Another unmarked police car had been roaming street to street and Ryan knew the chase was on. He knew the car as he had driven it.

Ryan knew the area and he knew which streets he could navigate around to reach the house without being detected. Just as he was getting closer to the house rounding a side street, a blue car stopped right alongside him, the door opened and a voice said, "Get in."

Tango had known the danger Detective Ryan Shad-Bolt had been in ever since he had helped her escape. She was also the master of disguises and as she had seen Ryan running, she knew she had to help him and then his family get out of the area.

"Get in, Ryan, we got to go."

"Tango, is that you?"

"Get in, Ryan, don't hesitate. The cops are just around the corner."

Ryan jumped in, closed the door and the car raced off.

"Tango, you look so different. Your hair, your face, your clothes."

"Ryan, there are checkpoint Charlies everywhere here in Australia, and now they will be looking for you."

"My family, I got to get them away."

"Ryan, we have already planned for them. An organised member dressed as a postman on a motor scooter met with your wife. He has explained everything and where she and the children must go in the next two hours, quietly and discreetly. She will be met in the park not far from your place and will be walking with someone who will be viewed as a friend. She has been told the police are watching her as they have had you under surveillance."

"And she believed the postman."

"He gave her a package with copies of falsified incriminating documents that the press were able to get a hold of about you. She's scared but she will do as asked. She and the children will be safe and you will meet up with them in one of the safe areas. In the meantime, put these on."

"What's this?"

"Jump suit, Ryan, we are going flying. You're ex-military and a paratrooper so I believe!"

The only place now free of the entertainment on the ground was in the air.

Foxtrot had arranged a light aircraft to take three parachutists and to fly out of the Brisbane Airways controlled area, flying enroute to Mackay. The drop zone was a farm just outside Mackay with three others. There would be a couple of landmarks to aim for on the farmer's airstrip.

A Holden Ute would be waiting to take all three to the safe house and tunnel entrance, arranged by Alpha. Alpha was still in Mackay and coordinating all the logistics with Lima and Zulu, Zulu having come back from WA and NSW after completing all the engineering inspections of tunnels and safe areas.

The community had grown strong, but there would always be one or two bad apples who thought they could run things better, not having a clue about the whole operation. These fellas were given an ultimatum: shape up or ship out. Any disgruntled person leaving would certainly want payback.

But the arrangement was if it came to that, they would be quickly sedated, removed, taken under nightfall and placed back where they came from.

All persons who were helped and needed helping under Alpha and the team's care would be checked out first. Foxtrot was able to access personal information on people and would discard it when the people who required help were genuine.

It was a win win for all.

Alpha had explained the very extreme challenges the world would come to face in the not-so-distant future.

The world had not learnt from the 2008 GFC.

From this, GFC ALHA had learnt the expression, "Beware of half-truths, you might have got the wrong half."

THE PLOT THICKENS

The flight from Brisbane to Mackay in a light single engine aircraft traveling at 130 kts true airspeed, not allowing for wind at 6000 feet, would be around three hours, a distance of four hundred and thirty-three nautical miles.

Tango was racing to get Ryan to Archerfield, the light aircraft airport out of Brisbane. Checkpoints were everywhere along the way. People were being tested for Covid, cars were being searched for persons associated with the Alpha team, and there was an APB out for Detective Ryan Shad-Bolt.

There were checkpoints set up for Covid but also as a cover to find Tango on the run. But Tango had no problem avoiding these checkpoints due to her excellent disguise. Ryan had a cap and sunglasses on. Wearing aviation overalls, he looked like air force aircrew with golden wings above the left pocket and a name on the right side.

At the last checkpoint just before reaching Archerfield, a young police officer stopped the car.

"Good morning, miss, we need some ID from both of you and you need to do a Covid check."

Tango replied, "We are in kind of a hurry to get to the airport. My friend here is flying an emergency run and we only have minutes. Departure time within the next ten to fifteen minutes. "

"Miss, just take this quick test and your ID is sufficient. The air force ID is sufficient as well, flight sergeant. Have a good day."

"Thanks, Officer."

Tango and Ryan couldn't wait to get from that checkpoint to Archerfield. Another five minutes and they would be pulling into the car park of a private hangar. There was no name on the hangar, but inside were office facilities, and a lounge.

The hangar itself housed three aircraft owned by one owner, Delta. Delta had this company operation for his clients in Queensland under a different company name for tax purposes.

ONE BEACH BARON, A CESSNA 210M, AND A LEAR JET 35.

The Lear Jet 35 was used across the country for top level business operations and Foxtrot was the chief pilot when not on duty with Qantas. Alpha also was the other pilot who was rated to fly the Lear 35 with Foxtrot.

Today Foxtrot had arrived from North Queensland to do a parachute drop on the southern side of Mackay. He had arrived especially to get Ryan and two others to a safe area. A parachute drop would be made in the C 210M from 6000 feet ASL on actual GPS coordinates.

Alpha had arranged with Jack Russell to pick them all up in a farm vehicle and bring them to the safe house. Ryan would also be re-united with his family there as Tango had promised.

Overnight the C210 had been fuelled up. A flight plan had been lodged with Airways Australia for a direct flight to Mackay and back, departing 2300 UTC (Universal Co-ordinated time), local time 10.00 a.m.

Foxtrot would drop them ten miles out on approach to Mackay airport. Everything had been planned to the last detail, but they didn't know Superintendent John Holland was checking all airports, including the light aircraft airports in the area and further north for planned activities from the Alpha team.

He had lost trace of Ryan, and his family had gone to the local park and never returned. A woman, supposedly his wife's friend, had come with her children and they had walked off together and not returned.

Foxtrot himself had to be called back on standby for active duty with Qantas and this meant some hours in the A320 Airbus simulator. He wasn't sure if he wanted to go back on flight duties.

"As the world gets crazier, the nuts get easier to find."

Foxtrot was now convinced his responsibilities lay elsewhere, and this environment with the Alpha team was more beneficial long term. The team had put together a plan under good guidance from one man's vision and years of planning and it had worked so far, with a little hiccup along the way.

The last part of the course needed to be fulfilled. The Alpha team knew they couldn't become complacent. They had to get everyone together in designated locations around the country with family and friends and ensure that those who joined the cause had nothing to lose.

Alpha and family were in Mackay, with Tango to join shortly. Lima and Foxtrot were also part of the North Queensland team. Charlie and Zulu remained hidden with their contingent of people in New South Wales, and Delta and Romeo with family and friends in WA.

The authorities didn't know what was going on.

Statements to the public were fake news.

Meanwhile, Alpha could not go back to the mining industry now as Ricky Martin. He was feeling the same as Foxtrot. The organisation had a big responsibility on their hands to keep families together. Alpha's family did not always understand the logic behind the operation and for a long time thought he was a conspiracist with all the information he had gathered off the internet. But as the world climate and the Covid crisis had a huge effect in the last year and a half, with countless irresponsible people and unfortunately stranded expats all over the world, a plan B did not seem too bad.

Alpha's wife and daughters had kept asking him questions about the way he had led this life. He had faced a number of setbacks when people or so-called friends had used him. Why did he let these things happen at the expense of having time with family and giving them his time and input into his young daughters' lives?

His youngest daughter asked, "Are you happy with life?"

Happy yes, but not having to work in an industry that was tough, long hours with the heat, the humidity, the travel. Like any other responsible parent, he had tried to do the best for his family at a considerable cost. But the tables were about to turn for Alpha.

Alpha had helped so many people over the years in mining, physically, emotionally, and talking through family concerns others were going through as he had gone through himself. In more ways than one, he was glad to be getting out of the industry now.

The Alpha team were heroes to the public but fugitives to the authorities.

The U.S. government were wanting answers. George Laban had to give an account of their failed takedown and no known leads, only small breaks in the case.

The police budget was well over any estimation.

The state and federal governments were having to deal with this ongoing Covid crisis and trying to keep businesses running, to keep people employed.

And of course, the Reserve bank was printing more currency. The more they printed, the more currencies around the world devalued.

THE DECOY

John Holland from Brisbane Central had been sent a flight plan from Airways Australia. A Beach Barron B58 flight was planned to Mackay at 2300hrs UTC. Four people were on board.

"I want that plane and pilot searched as it lands at Mackay airport," said John Holland. "We may not have Alpha, but we will have one or two of his team," he said with a sadistic smile on his face. "And I want to be there this time at the airport. Everyone, gather round. I want checkpoints in and out of Mackay Airport, I want teams of foot patrols in the streets of the Mackay CBD, and I want checkpoints from the South and the North of Mackay. Alpha, we are coming to take you down."

What Superintendent John Holland didn't realise, the Beach Baron light twin engine aircraft was a decoy. The passengers were businessmen who had chartered the aircraft as a returning home flight. The pilot was a company pilot for Delta's operation in Queensland.

Foxtrot had loaded the C210M with his parachutists to be dropped off as planned to the farm station. His flight plan would be a milk run with stop off places on the way with freight. That's what they call a milk run. Ryan and the two other fellas, Phil and Paul, would be seated on the floor with their parachutes on in a ready state, and they themselves concealed. Not the most comfortable of places to be in.

As far as airways Australia knew, the flight plan was for a scheduled freight run. And yes it was, with a few extra drop offs along the way. Foxtrot would not land in Mackay but would divert to Proserpine Airport refuel and fly back to Brisbane without anyone knowing his real cargo.

"Ryan, Paul, Phil, pack your gear in, we are leaving. We got a time frame of dropping you all off over the drop off point. I need you all to keep your heads low, this flight is planned as a freight run and I'm flying this route today as a relief pilot. The police will be waiting at the Mackay airport for the Beach Baron to arrive, apprehending the pilot Joey Beach and his passengers, who will give the impression that they are extremely upset businessmen, who for no reason have been taken into police custody."

Foxtrot went through all the pre-start and then the start-up checks of the C210M. Radios were briefed by Brisbane ground for clearance to Proserpine direct. A taxi clearance was then issued by Archerfield tower with all readbacks in radio communications correct.

With pre-take-off checks and then lining up of runway 04 and with a wind direction of 350 degrees true, a take-off clearance was given from the tower, with airborne instructions climbing through 800ft to contact Brisbane centre. The C210M would climb to 6000 ft and then level off.

Foxtrot would write down every clearance, passing time to every way point and having all his navigation radios tuned into navigation beacons along the way. Also, his GPS was set to way points and the final drop off point for the jump.

The sky was blue, a typical picture of Queensland this time of year.

All the boys in the back of the aircraft with their chutes on was a picture. They sat back-to-back with their eyes closed.

Foxtrot turned around and a verse from Isaiah out of the Bible came to him.

"But those who trust in the Lord will find new strength. They will soar on wings like eagles; they will run and not grow weary, they will walk and not faint."

Foxtrot had a faith and he knew above all that was happening, the Alpha team were trying to save lives, not destroy lives as Covid was doing. People were looking for hope, not political correctness and confusion.

All the authorities were trying to do was stop a change in their system which they couldn't control and it was now out of hand.

John Holland and George Laban were out for blood and were looking for someone or some organisation to take down, which happened to be the Alpha team, but nothing had seemed to work for them.

The people of Australia and those who had been watching current events around the world had been exposed to the truth, with the cover ups from banking systems, political gains for politicians. But amongst these politicians were those who were fighting for the people as well. There is good and bad on both sides and at least Australia and NZ had stable governments.

The real problem was the corruption of world politics and those that were setting up a new world order. The Alpha team were making a stand against it and the great reset coming on the global finance.

"The riders of the apocalypse had come." Revelation 6:1-10.

The White Horseman was armed with a bow. This is Christ and the bow represents God's Covenant just like the rainbow he gave to Noah as a promise. The covenant was that Christ will restore all creation.

When the second seal is opened by Christ, the second horseman, a fiery red one came out and he was given power to take peace from the earth and make people kill each other. A large sword came out. (The wars that have plagued the world, with more in recent times).

The Bible says the harmony of peace was given in creation in Genesis 1:31.

The third seal is opened and a black horseman rode out with a set of scales in his hand. Revelation 6:5

The scales represent the everyday buying and selling. These

scales however are rigged to increase the cost of grain. The third horseman represents economic injustice, robbing people of their daily bread and other basic needs. God hates injustice.

A day's wages for a small bag of grain or flower would have an impact on their survival. (The catastrophic effect on businesses and layoffs around the world due to Covid, the diminishing economies). God knows the importance of daily bread for everyone.

The fourth seal was opened and a pale horseman, and its rider was named death.

The fourth horseman is too familiar, maybe you have felt the pain and grief disrupting your lives.

May you be comforted by God's love and care.

This, at the point of the Covid crisis which has killed over two million people and is ongoing.

The fifth seal was opened and under the altar the souls that had been martyred for the word of God and their testimony. (Take a look at the persecutions in the last century, China, North Korea, Muslim countries, Africa). Standing for who you believe in is a testimony.

Foxtrot was not thinking of the events as mentioned as gloom, but being in the right place at the right time. He with the Alpha team were making a stand against injustice.

The C210M was making good time to pass over drop off point. The sky was clear all the way up the eastern seaboard. Mackay is coastal, Proserpine to the north of Mackay was inland and the gateway to the Whit Sundays a tropical paradise.

"Drop zone coming up, fellas," said Foxtrot.

Foxtrot had received clearance through the Mackay control zone enroute to Proserpine, having called up at a designated reporting point to the south of Mackay, maintaining 6000 feet. The control zone covered a radius of twenty nautical miles and Foxtrot was flying on a VFR flight plan as the day was clear and the drop off point could be visualised due to the favourable weather conditions.

The door was opened on the C210M. Ryan was ready to go first.

"Overhead now," shouted Foxtrot.

Out jumped Ryan, followed by Paul and Phil. Three images descended and their chutes opened as soon as they were clear of aircraft. For safety reasons, a pilot dropping off parachutists always carried a chute just in case of parachutists' entanglement around flight control as of aircraft.

Foxtrot was within thirty minutes to Proserpine airport and on descent. On the descent, there was a loud bang. An engine oil line had broken and the engine was losing oil pressure fast. If Foxtrot didn't shut the engine down quickly, it would seize.

He was within ten nautical miles from the Proserpine Airport now and had to set the aircraft up into the forced landing profile with no power.

The aircraft was a piston engine, fuel injected with no carburetor.

A quick assessment and then he went through the emergency checks.

Height, not less than 3000 feet. Foxtrot was through 5000 feet.

Gear up, flaps up, aircraft trimmed up and holding at 70 kts.

Foxtrot couldn't warm the engine as he had selected the mixture lever to off and fuel to off.

This was a forced landing with no power.

Proserpine Airport was in range to make the landing. The wind direction Foxtrot had established by smoke and cloud shadow in the area was from the north east. He could set up his 1500 foot mark at ninety degrees on the right-hand side of runway 14 with the 1000 foot mark at ninety degrees to runway 32. Foxtrot would need to land on runway 32.

Foxtrot mayday checks would be the next priority.

"Mayday, mayday, mayday. Proserpine traffic echo whiskey lima Cessna 210M approaching three miles from the south with an engine failure. Will be joining over head to land on runway 32."

There had been a Qantas 737 on approach. It heard the mayday call and immediately acknowledged the call. The captain made the decision to climb up into the hold above Proserpine, as emergency traffic have right of way. He would attempt the approach again when the runways cleared or he was diverted to Mackay.

Foxtrot then proceeded to make sure fuel was off and all electrics were off except for the master switch, which remained on. He needed to be able to lower landing gear and flap on final approach, when he was sure he was going to make the landing on runway 32.

Foxtrot was now at his 1500 foot mark, a little high but he could lose that height as he proceeded to the 1000 foot mark. Better to be high than too low. If too low on final approach, he would undershoot the runway, and if it was too high, he had enough length on runway to compensate for.

Foxtrot was able to maintain the 70 to 75 kts in the glide. He had set up a reasonably good approach.

Foxtrot had heard the acknowledgement of the captain of the Qantas 737 and other commuter aircraft in the vicinity, and was immediately looking for a safe area to run the C210 off after landing.

He had now turned on the final approach on runway 32 with the gear down and twenty degrees of flap, airspeed holding. The runway now was meters away and he saw a flat area he could quickly turn off and run onto when landing. Foxtrot wouldn't need to use his breaks as the momentum of the plane and the turning onto the grass area would slow him down to stop the aircraft.

A perfect landing was made and he steered the aircraft onto the grass area to the side of runway. The C210M came to a stop.

An emergency vehicle raced out and Foxtrot realised how his professional skills had prevented a serious accident. He turned and closed his eyes and quietly said thank you.

There would be a full investigation by the Australian Civil Aviation authority with paperwork to follow.

Foxtrot had achieved his mission, as all three parachutists had landed safely. A phone call on an old cell phone with no GPS tracking was had confirmed it. The men were on their way to meet their families at the appropriate safe houses.

The station manager had had everything ready at the pickup point inland from Mackay. He too had been grateful for the help of the Alpha team who had helped his struggling farm in the Covid crisis.

He had struggled to get workers. The Alpha team had come up with a solution that helped make his farm produce viable crops. They had given the farmer some of their ready hands to harvest tropical fruits and vegetables.

Alpha, with the help once again from team effort, had safely secured another three families.

Meanwhile in Mackay, the Beach Baron had landed. Joe and his passengers were ready for the police confrontation and would act surprised.

Parking in the light aircraft area and shutting down the engines, the federal police arrived in full force.

George Laban was there, shouting, "This is a federal investigation and all of you on this flight are being taken into custody to answer a number of questions and help with the police enquiries."

From the local businessmen came some put-on protest, asking, "What is this all about and under whose authority do you have the right to do this?"

"No questions will be answered without a lawyer present," shouted one of the men.

"Take all four, I want them briefed down at the Mackay station," said George Laban.

The frustrations were about to play on George Laban again as he had this feeling he had been foiled once more. With the wrong people in custody, he could have a lawsuit with police harassment being the topic on a legal case.

But one play a federal police commander can make is the claim that "it was all in the national interests, even if I got it wrong."

Yes, there would be an enquiry, but tracking the Alpha team down was his priority.

Every day the state premier and prime minister's office had wanted a report on progress. George would have to carefully select his words. He could not say they still had no evidence or suspects but they were working on a number of leads. In effect, George and the state police had come to a stalemate, not quite a checkmate, as Alpha wanted to play his last card.

Alpha knew that time was running out for the authorities and the expense of chasing the Alpha team down was running into the millions. Covid had taken its toll and still was. The federal government support was running out, to thousands who had lost work and those who were working in heavy industries were paying heavy taxes.

There was a big crisis coming worldwide and to the unsuspecting, this would be the final blow.

Alpha had been reminded of an industrialist during World War II in Europe. He had made profits for supplying the German war machine with arms. He realised the people in the factories were Jewish families, imprisoned as slaves by the Nazis from the concentration camps nearby. These people became his friends and many others wanted to be part of his factory workers as he protected them from the brutality of the Nazis. Towards the closing of the war, he was having his Jewish accountant write up lists and lists of all the people he could think of to prevent from being sent away to other extermination camps. Oskar Schindler was actually buying with his own wealth the lives of his workers from the Nazis and at the same time producing defective arms for the Germans.

He became a hero to Israel and effectively, with the thousand or more lives he saved, their offspring numbered over five thousand. Losing his wealth didn't mean much to Oskar but saving lives did. At the very end, he broke down, thinking he could have saved many more lives, but was comforted by those around him whose lives he had saved.

Alpha knew from sponsoring children in three continents of the world over many years that he could save more families in a crisis.

The team had the resources, infrastructure and expertise that was dwindling for the opposition trying to hunt him and the team down.

George Laban had flown into a rage as the plane and passengers he had impounded were indeed a business aircraft and legitimate business owners and they were not happy.

George wanted to search the hangar and office where that plane had taken off. When he found out who the owner of the charter company and buildings was, he was more puzzled.

Jimmy Swaggart (Delta) from WA owned the business and the building in Queensland. George did not know Jimmy's code name, but knew of him as a very wealthy engineering contractor who had influence in the WA state government.

There were three aircraft hangered in this hangar. The Lear 35 was here, the Beach Baron had been impounded in Mackay, but there was another plane not there.

George had the Airways Australia flight plans checked to find a C210M, which had flown a milk run earlier in the day. The pilot had called an emergency, making a forced landing at Proserpine airport, inland from the Whitsundays.

George was still in Mackay. He could get a police chopper to fly him to Proserpine.

"I want the pilot of that aircraft stopped and interviewed till I can get there," said George Laban.

Foxtrot had dealt with the emergency services, advised the Civil Aviation Safety Authority of the incident, and would leave the C210M parked where it was, out of the way of traffic and for the CAA to do a full investigation. His details were those of the hangar and he certainly would be interviewed.

But Foxtrot knew if he was interviewed by Civil Aviation Safety

Authority, the feds would be onto him as well. So being picked up in the car park at Proserpine airport, he chose to remain anonymous for a bit. Foxtrot's real name was on the flight plan and the federal police would go looking. The address he had given was the hangar and the company phone was left in the hangar office intentionally. As he and Tango were leaving Proserpine Airport, the federal police came screaming in with sirens blazing.

Tango and Foxtrot had left just in time. They were now on their way to one of the safe houses to join the others and their families.

Ryan with Phil and Paul had been dropped off by the farm manager to a street name and number they were given. They had changed from their jump suits to casual clothes and looked pre-sentable and less conspicuous.

A gate was automatically opened. There was a person standing on the other side of the gate waiting for them. The three male gents were greeted accordingly.

It was then that Ryan and the others were taken through and downstairs under the safe house to meet up with their families with Lima.

The two had been protected and were happy to see their spouses.

Ryan, not a man to shed emotion, was overwhelmed with what he saw.

These safe houses had been wonderfully set up to meet all the needs of those who inhabited them. There was nothing dismal about them and when he was told of all the provisions the Alpha team had acquired from building necessary tunnels to harbour all necessary items to protect them from coming events, Ryan could not believe this was possible.

Ryan and his wife were told the same provisions had been set up not only in Queensland, but NSW, WA, and a few other satellite areas.

Lima had made sure the security of all premises had kept everyone secure. There was the back entrance to each tunnel from the properties that were secured and not visible to prying eyes. This gave adequate movement for people to quietly come and go.

if you don't take risks, you'll always be working for someone who does.

George Laban had arrived at Proserpine Airport. And the C210M had been cordoned off by police tape. The feds had been able to override CASA, as this involved a national police investigation.

What was he carrying on this flight as there seemed to be no evidence of any consignments or packages going to outback stations? What was he doing here and where was the pilot?

George and his team had been down this track many times before. They had never been able to find the pilot. He simply vanished.

In WA, at Geraldton Port, a consignment on a ship from Turkey had simply disappeared.

They had lost the only contact with the Alpha team member "Tango."

Detective Ryan Shad-Bolt and his family had disappeared.

He had impounded the wrong aircraft and occupants at the Mackay Airport and he himself could be facing legal charges for aiding and abetting an escaped suspect.

The tunnels found were bogus tunnels and the real ones were never found.

And they had a plane with no pilot who could have been the only clue and had now vanished.

"Who is this Alpha and his team? What are they so adamantly preparing for?"

The Civil Aviation Safety Authority would be interested in the pilot and the cause of engine failure only and the plane would be taken away and hangered and eventually a new engine installed.

Tango and Foxtrot had arrived at the other safe house in Mackay with Alpha and his family.

Alpha's good friend and flying buddy had made it.

The efforts in the air and on the ground with his computer skills had a tremendous impact on everything that had been planned.

Everyone was together although in different parts of the country. All preparations now and ongoing for future events were in place.

Zulu and Charlie were in New South Wales. Delta and Romeo were in WA, Romeo was out of quarantine running the Western Australia side. (Romeo had brought his sister to Perth to take care of her. She was recovering from the severity of the hit and run incident.) A small team was running in Victoria and South Australia.

The biggest thank you would go to the above higher power whose world we live in and his promises are sure.

George Logan was near conceding to defeat. There was only camera footage of a couple leaving the terminal in a car going south. The number plate could be vaguely seen. But the registration was enough to check the Queensland car registration of road transport.

The plates had been de-registered weeks ago as the car had been supposedly scrapped.

How can a car have been brought back to life again when it has been de-registered and scrapped? George thought. The last owner was an old lady who had passed away months before.

Whilst the federal police and state police were desperately trying to take the Alpha team down, George and Cyril had not been paying attention to the world financial events.

The share markets had skyrocketed in weeks around the world. An international false economy due to Covid was being propped up. People were sick and dying, many others were living in fear.

The crash would be tremendous when it happened.

Alpha hadn't given up on many other families that were struggling. With the food resources from the farming areas, the farmers were carefully stockpiling—on Alpha's insistence—vegetables, fruits, meats, poultry, and grain, anything that would help humanity in times of adversity.

Insecure people are self-absorbed. If you're self-absorbed, you will never add value.

Was Alpha doing something for someone who would not be able to repay him?

When you invest in people, you will never know what the returns are going to be.

Not only was the Alpha team gearing up for a disaster and literally saving lives but also trying to add or give mentorship in a time of crisis and build up more leaders the world so desperately needed. It was no hideaway from society. This was investing in people, their families, their God-given abilities.

Why couldn't those who were supposed to be in leadership positions give quality mentorship and be good stewards of the resources they had been entrusted with?

Unfortunately, there is a time of reckoning coming for all of us. It could be tomorrow, next week, next year.

And as the Bible says in Daniel 5:27, "You have been weighed, you have been measured, and you have been found wanting."

Don't be found wanting.

"Worry weighs a person down; an encouraging word cheers a person up." Proverbs 12:25

The Alpha team had joined together as a band of brothers and sisters to encourage not discourage the people they so cared for.

THE BIG FINANCIAL CRASH

The past cannot be changed, edited, or erased. It can only be accepted. What you learn from it gives you more power to move on and do better.

The world would say, "You need this. This will make your life easier for you. You need this to lose weight and look like this. You buy now, pay now later." The unfortunate thing about the pay later, it comes with a high price tag. Instead of pay now play later, or delayed gratification, people in the western society have built false economies with instant gratification.

And the day of reckoning has come.

It was a Friday night. Stocks and commodities on the international share markets were being sold off at a phenomenal rate. It couldn't be slowed down, and people were panicking. Watching the news, people were flooding to the banks to get their currency out, but the currency itself had devalued to a point it was just paper or figures and the banks did not have enough of it. It was more electronic figures.

The governments around the world had just kept printing to oblivion, hoping to bail the situation out. But this time it didn't work.

A flash back in history to Germany in the 1920s, the German people were carrying barrel loads of currency to buy over inflated items. It went from a hyper deflation to a hyperinflation, causing the Great Depression in 1929 till the early 1930s around the world.

Will we keep blaming others for our incompetence? Or should

we have learnt from history what works and what doesn't?

The Alpha team had prepared for this, Alpha over the last ten years. This weekend and into the next week onwards would leave George Laban and Superintendent John Holland in disarray. They would now have more to deal with in real criminal activities and besides George Laban legal issues against him, having arrested falsely two businessmen and a pilot on circumstantial evidence.

Alpha and the team had won the chess game. Checkmate. There was no way George and John Holland could take down the Alpha team now, as many would try to find help from Alpha and team to give them assistance.

This had been Alpha's plan all along.

The world was broken overnight. People in many countries would lose everything they had valued.

The sad part about it was people had placed values on the wrong things. "Money and assets, not people."

The Alpha team had placed "value on people and treating people fairly."

Everyone with the Alpha team, and there were many now, had been rescued from many of life's ordeals and were just happy to thank God that they and their families were safe.

This would not stop the unruliness to come but this was a reprieve and they would be able to survive till the master of the universe would take them home.

The value of basic foods and essentials would skyrocket now. A day's wages for a loaf of bread.

The farmers now would have to be on their guard. And many who lived in rural areas who were self-sufficient would also need to protect their assets.

The farmers who had been working with Alpha had stored enough food to last for them and their neighbours, Alpha's team and friends for the next three years. It would take a period of time for the world to replenish its resources.

"TO WHOM MUCH IS GIVEN,
MUCH WILL BE REQUIRED. "
—Luke 12:48

We are held responsible for what we have. If we have been blessed with talents, wealth, knowledge, time and the like, it is expected we benefit others.

People who had foolishly looked to those in governments would be bitterly disappointed as the governments had no answers to fix the problems and unfortunately, a world leader would come onto the scene who would look to fix all the world's problems.

The American economy had collapsed under the weak administration, to many Americans' anger.

Adolph Hitler rose to power under the same circumstances in the 1930s. The German people were starving, the Weimar government had nearly collapsed and the German people looked to him or should I say succumbed to him to be led into one of the vilest parts of history.

So the story of the Alpha team would rise above government intervention to help and aid those who chose and not those who would become bitter and resentful.

Alpha, a quiet unassuming fella with his family, team and friends, had pulled off a daring mission to save the lives of hundreds maybe thousands of people and not only had they stored treasures that would one day be part of a new government established by the owner of this world but they would bring an influence of the goodness of our creator. We cannot outgive him, but what he blesses us with we must pass on to others.

It's in the act of giving that we see lives changed.

The Covid crisis had been only the beginning of the world crisis. But there was hope because there were other Alpha groups who had taken up the challenge, not to fix the world's problems, but they had been resourceful in stockpiling the basic necessities to live on over time. These organisations had a band of brothers and sisters to who had laid their lives on the line to take in those who chose to be free from a world crisis.

The Alpha Team continues their story and the challenges they face, with a one world order, who they refuse to acknowledge, as every country has to maintain its God-given sovereignty.

The federal and state police could not continue the chase on the Alpha Team as the police budgets now were nearly non-existent. And George Laban, John Holland, Cyril Bradwell to their disgust had other priorities. Even keeping their own jobs was a priority.

The Australian resources and agricultural industries were still holding a fledging economy only just.

The state of the nation was in panic mode, with bank mortgage sales nationwide, repossession of goods, cars, toys.

The Alpha team had risen out of the ashes to help protect the sovereignty of the Australian nation. The price of freedom had come at a cost and had nearly been lost to those world conspirators that had an agenda.

Those who had sworn to protect the public had now found themselves sworn to protect a corporation. The Australian people had now woken to the cause. The Alpha team had triggered that cause.

Watch in the next series what the Alpha Team and all those behind him do, to keep Australia and New Zealand two sovereign countries.

Australian National Anthem

Australians, all let us rejoice
for we are young and free
we've golden soil and wealth for toil
our home is girt by sea
our land abounds in nature's gifts
of beauty rich and rare
in history's page let every stage
advance Australia fair.

New Zealand National Anthem

God of nations at thy feet
In the bonds of love we meet
Here our voices, we entreat
God defend our free land
Guard Pacific's triple star
From the shafts of strife and war
Make her praises heard afar
God defend New Zealand

E IHOWA ATUA
O NGA IWI MATOU RA
ATA WHAKARANGONA
me AROHA NOA
KIA HUA KO TE PAI
KIA TAU to ATAWHAI
manAAKitIA MAI
AOTEAROA

This story is fictional
but there are true factual events
which follow through.

Richard J Stewart

————————————

FREEDOM IN ANY CASE
IS ONLY POSSIBLE BY
CONSTANTLY STRUGGLING FOR IT
—Albert Einstein

www.ingramcontent.com/pod-product-compliance
Lightning Source LLC
Chambersburg PA
CBHW020522120726
47904CB00003B/940